An Empire of Silence
A Story about a Crime

Anthony Chapman

Acknowledgements

I have quoted from the following song,

'Mammas, Don't Let Your Babies Grow Up To Be Cowboys,' written by E Bruce and P Bruce

I also wish to acknowledge Wikipedia

An Empire of Silence

Copyright © 2014 Fergus Anthony Chapman

All rights reserved.

ISBN-10: 149431102X
ISBN-13: 978 – 1494311025

Cover art: Child Crying by Anthony Chapman.
For more visit www.fergusanthony.com

To all writers whose books, like this
skirt the ridiculous,
and sometimes cross over.

More importantly:

To my brother Kieran
who started promoting this book
on Facebook while it was still being edited.

NOTE

This story began as a screenplay during July/August 2001. It was called Enigma – nothing to do with the code machine. I turned it into a novel in 2005. Since then, a Charles Bronson movie called *The Mechanic*, mentioned in these pages, has been remade. The remake is great fun, but I recommend the original.

An Empire of Silence

*Believe we are born
To live simply and with love
In the world at hand*

            Peter Hopkins

Peter Hopkins – I

One day, when he was twelve years of age, Peter Hopkins went to play in the attic of his grandparents' house. His imagination transformed that dead space into a living temple filled with ancient treasures. Boxes carrying the insignia of Brillo, Fyffe's, and Campbell's, held the keys to a past that, his grandfather assured him, was better than anything life could ever offer the young boy. Through the eyes of an antique gas mask, he saw himself safely through the trenches of World War 1. Slashing wildly with an old epée, stolen from the local drama group, he cut a dash through the stagnant air and pinned a dusty hardback to the floor. The book was a collection of poetry by Lord Byron, and standing in the settling dust, the boy felt his lips curl into a smile, as he read the legend: *Mad, Bad and Dangerous to Know.*

Peter knelt to pick the book up; he noticed the smell of the paper. This was not a new sensation, but for the first time, the fragrance charged his mind with wild imaginings. He began to read. The rhythm of the words enlivened the shadows inside the attic. At the same time, Peter felt a space around him; he felt he was moving differently, experiencing life differently. For the first time, Peter had a sense that he was himself. He turned the page and trembled at the title: *Don Juan.*

Don Juan was a name Peter had known for years. Of all he possessed what possessed him most was a black and white photograph of himself as a baby. He is caught in mid bounce on his grandfather's knee, with the old man dressed as the mythical lover: Don Juan at sixty-five. To a boy on the brink of puberty, with all its attendant uncertainty, the discovery of the poem conjured up a life far removed from anything he had ever known; it promised a life of adventure, filled with heroic deeds. A sudden inspiration told Peter that poetry would be a good way to win women's hearts. Poetry would set him on the road to fame, but not as a poet. He imagined himself as the kind of man who walks into the jungle with nothing but his guts, to return years later, changed but untamed, possessor of secret knowledge, blood brother to unknown tribes who, having escaped the ravages of civilization, still lived in harmony with creation.

That night, with a flashlight, pen and exercise book, Peter took a new kind of nervousness to bed. Beneath the covers, he began to write, copying the style of Byron, but the results, he was certain, were trash. After a few days, he quit, but the work was in him now, and he soon found himself back beneath the bedclothes, pen in hand, struggling with the syntax, fighting words. He discovered and discarded Charles Bukowski in a week. He passed through Yeats like a dream. Dickinson confused him. He developed a system: every Sunday night he would copy a poem into his exercise book. Over the course of the week, he'd change a word here and there, but leave the structure intact. He'd repeat this process until he felt the work before him was his own. In this way, he amassed some fifty poems over the course of the year. However, anyone can do that, what he needed was publication. Who could then deny that he was something special?

In keeping with his romantic vision, he searched for a bookshop that reeked of history, uneven shelves heavy with unpronounceable names, the ceiling stained with cigarette smoke, and the dust of generations in the air. He found *Books Upstairs,* a shop that occupied two floors above a greengrocer. He loved the staircase that climbed from one floor to the next, the stacks of books to the side of each step. About half way up, a flattened cigarette butt bore the partial imprint of the sole of a work boot. As Peter entered the top floor of the shop, the smell of fresh biscuits, and the cigarette smoke dancing in the dusty sun made his head swim. A small crowd sat spellbound, watching a man make spastic noises that no one could understand. After a few minutes, he stopped and said, "I've been thinking about the word 'Daybreak', and of all the implied violence in that word. 'The day,' has been, 'broken.' We need, to 'fix', 'the day'. This next piece is entitled 'Fixing the Day'." He cleared his throat and began again, making the same spastic noises that no one understood.

Peter went back downstairs. He poured over the shelves, looking for a magazine that cried poverty with the greatest authenticity. He searched for an hour and found a slim homemade book with a light blue craft paper cover. A photocopied ballpoint pen drawing of an open window invited readers to explore *The UniVerse*. He opened the book and found the work of twenty poets spread over fifty photocopied pages; this was the kind of magazine taken seriously in the ranks of rebellion.

He submitted his poems and followed their journey through the post, to the manicured hands of a woman with blood-red fingernails and a perfect hourglass figure. His work would penetrate all her hidden places and pierce her heart. She would wet herself and know that she had to have him. She would be *Parisienne*, of course. This did not necessarily mean she came from Paris. In his Geography of flesh, being *Parisienne* located her in some elevated 'other' place: a world of sexual and intellectual sophistication. He felt her call to him, and he knew that, through her, his life would begin.

In due course, his work returned with corrections. There was a note from the editor, congratulating the young poet on his choice of reading. He recommended other books that would help Peter to develop and to discover his own voice. The letter had been signed by a man. Sitting on his bed, staring at the signature, Peter began to doubt the existence of *Parisienne* women.

For a long time afterward he did not write a word, but the term 'find your voice' had stirred something up. His next attempt at poetry was for the thing itself. He wanted to see where the words would lead.

01/A Burglary in Winter

Sheets of lightning pulsed in the sky, brightening the bellies of fat clouds and lighting up the battlements of the Whitely Museum: an old English castle that had been transported to the New England countryside. Here and there, patches of frost sparkled like glitter on the walls, and recent rain caused the slate roofs to shine silver in the night. At a short distance, a freeway ran along what had once been part of the Whitely Estate, and just inside the perimeter wall, Jack Higgins, crouching in a copse of trees, waited and watched.

He was there to steal the Whitely Diamond and to leave irrefutable proof of the break-in. This was for the benefit of the outside world. No one must be allowed to deny the theft had taken place. Under ordinary circumstances, he would never do this. To Jack, burglary was an art form, and the victims of his art should discover the theft only after exhausting every other possibility.

A flash of lightning showed two guards, keeping perfect time, complete a circuit of the building. Their rain ponchos cast ghoulish shadows against the castle wall. They stopped to talk to each other. A ribbon of flame leapt from a Zippo as one of the guards lighted a cigarette. For a moment, Jack was aware only of the glow from the cigarettes. He felt the ghost of a craving, the pull of smoke in his mouth. He smiled; their habit might prove useful if he had to make a run for it. Their cigarettes finished; the guards moved off in opposite directions. Jack set his stopwatch and sat with the countdown until the guards should meet at the far side of the castle. Then, like a fighter about to step into the ring, he pushed aside everything but his immediate task. There would be time enough later to reflect, relaxing on the terrace of his penthouse in the sun, sipping a glass of Tullamore Dew, and watching the ships in the Gulf of Mexico.

He petitioned the stained-glass saints in the windows to watch over him, and walked quickly to the castle wall. He turned to face the battlements and began to climb.

On the roof, Jack hunkered down to get his bearings. He uncoiled a length of high tensile wire from around his waist and fixed it to the wall, ready for his escape. He moved along to the section of roof through which he would enter the castle. He removed about twenty slates and put them to one side. Then he cut a hole in the roofing felt, snipped through a layer of chicken wire, and lowered himself into the attic. He crawled along the rafters to a ring of one-inch steel bars. These were directly above the diamond and set to slam down at any change in pressure on the pedestal below. The bars were six inches apart, making a circle four feet in diameter. One of those bars would have to be removed.

Jack stood up and took his gloves off. He felt along the top of the steel ring that held the bars in place. He found a slight depression on top of one of the bars and marked it with a piece of chalk. He took a small metal box from his jacket pocket and left it on the rafter above the bar. He put his gloves back on.

In the room below, soft white powder fell from the ceiling and lightly dusted one of the most celebrated jewels in American history: the Whitely Diamond, the famous blood diamond from which the family fortune flowed. Moments later, a few centimeters of a fiber-optic camera peeped unnoticed through a hole that was barely there.

Jack pushed a button on the monitor in his hand. The screen lit up with a night-vision image of the Whitely

Diamond, almost invisible against the white velvet cushion on which it sat. Turning the camera, he caught sight of a marble bust, depicting honor, courage, compassion, and integrity. These qualities, chiseled into the face of the first American Whitely, told nothing of the man himself. As he watched the image, Jack heard the slow, steady rhythm of footsteps approaching. Moments later, the screen turned white as the lights in the Diamond Room came on when the guard entered. Jack pushed another button on the monitor and once again had a clear image. He watched the Guard circle the diamond and leave.

Jack withdrew the fiber optic. He widened the hole just enough to take a thin metal tube. Through this, he lowered a series of hooks that opened out and gripped the ceiling, holding the tube in place. He attached an arm to the tube. At the end of the arm was a blade, with which Jack now began to cut a hole in the ceiling of the Diamond Room. This was the most dangerous part of the job; tedious work threatening to lull him into autopilot while his nerves were eager for action. He worked for almost an hour, one slow, shallow circle at a time. The heat in the attic was made more oppressive by the close quarters. He had to stop several times to wipe his face, and once to wait for the guard to circle the diamond and leave. Before the final cut came the sound of the guard making another round.

After the guard had left, Jack wrapped a rope around the bar he had selected. He stood up and rolled his shoulders, then opened the metal box he had left on the rafter. He took a vial of acid from the box and squeezed a few drops into the depression at the top of the bar. The attic filled with smoke, too thick for a torch to penetrate. Jack crouched down and picked up the end of the rope. He gently tugged until the bar began to move. A few more tugs and the bar broke free. He stood motionless for several seconds and listened for any sounds from below. He felt the silence as a something tangible. He put the bar to one side, fixed his harness to the rafters and lifted the lid on the treasure trove below.

After squeezing into the confines of the outdated security system, Jack pushed a button on his chest. He dropped eight feet through the hole and found himself trapped in a glass case that surrounded the diamond from floor to ceiling. This had not been visible on the monitor. It had not been mentioned in the brief. He threw a thought away and refocused on the job. He reached out and picked the jewel from its white velvet cushion.

Steel doors slammed shut; an alarm sounded, echoing around the room, calling down the corridor, startling the guards into action. The steel bars slammed down around Jack and sent a shudder of prison through his body. A bar brushed his right shoulder and Jack dropped the diamond. For a brief, terrifying eternity, his breath stopped, his eyes froze, his world telescoped into the sight of the falling stone. Swinging around, Jack caught it in his boots. Cradling it there for a moment, he began to breathe again. The steel door struggled to open, years of neglect slowed the mechanism. Still, a guard was in under the door and firing by the time Jack had stuffed the diamond inside his jacket. Armed guards were another thing the brief had omitted. In an explosion of glass and noise, a bullet flew past Jack and ricocheted off one of the steel bars that surrounded him. He swung round, struggling to stay focused. He pulled a grenade from his jacket and tossed it to the guard, who, on reflex, caught it. In a fit of panic, he realized what it was and threw it away. He dived for cover as a small explosion filled the room with smoke. Within this cloud, Jack pushed the button on his chest and was reeled back into the attic, leaving behind the confused sound of security guards unused to dealing with an actual security breach.

There were pools of light floating in the sky. The entire estate was lit up. Jack climbed out into the night. The storm was growing. Ten feet away, electricity flowered from the lightning rod on the roof of the castle. Loud banging to his left turned Jack's attention to the roof access door, also suffering from lack of use. A sudden small explosion of dust and broken slate caused Jack to drop down onto his stomach. Just as he registered what was happening, the shot rang out – bullets travel faster than sound. The heavens opened, and rain hammered down. Still on his stomach, Jack crawled to where he had left the high tensile wire. He sat up, flat against the wall, and pulled a small black box from inside his jacket, raised a short aerial and pushed a button. A series of explosions around the castle brought darkness and cover. Jack listened as the guards scrambled confused towards that diversion. He scouted the ground for any guards still waiting. There were two. Their guns were holstered and they were vigilantly watching everywhere but the roof. There seemed little to choose between them. Jack launched himself off the roof, swinging out and down in a wide arc. His feet touched the wall, and he had kicked off again by the time the wire reached the ground. The two guards turned their heads towards the monster that was falling from the sky. One of the guards fumbled, trying to draw his gun. In almost the same instant, Jack was on his man and together they tumbled painfully to the ground. The other guard raised his gun and pointed it roughly in Jack's direction; he squeezed the trigger. Nothing happened. The guard looked at the weapon as if it were an alien device in his hands. Then he remembered the safety catch.

Jack rolled with the guard he had landed on, positioning the guard on top of him. The gun in the other guards hand went off, spraying bullets into the sky and raining panic down on the freeway. A knee to the groin caused the guard on top of Jack to jerk upright. Then with both feet, Jack pushed him to his companion, who had thrown his gun away when it roared so violently.

Jack got to his feet, grabbed the discarded gun and ran for the trees. The head of security released a Rottweiler.

The dog bounded past the other guards. Jack fired a short burst of gunfire in their direction. It bought him a few seconds, enough to reach the wall, enough, almost, to escape. He had just grabbed the top of the wall when he felt a powerful force close on his boot. With every ounce of strength left to him, Jack fought against the dog that was trying to pull him to the ground. The guards were almost on top of him now. The head of security barked at the others, warning that there would be hell to pay if anyone shot Satan. Consequently, the guards took pains to fire into the ground well away from the dog.

The dog began to win, forcing Jack to give up part of his grip on the wall. He reached for the gun swinging at his side, found it and emptied the clip into the dog's head. It exploded in a mixture of blood, bone, and brain. Jack disappeared over the wall with Satan's jaws still locked around his boot.

The head of security stopped. He stood, lost, empty, a world away from the chaos around him. Someone had murdered his best friend. He raised his gun; his finger closed around the trigger, firing blindly as he walked to the remains of his dog. He stood for a moment in grief, turning obscenities over in his head, but he had been raised correctly, and they never passed his lips. He tried to follow Jack over the wall. But after years of nursing his ass into obesity, all the Guard had left were the pains in his heart, one for the effort, and one for his love.

The other guards, their prey out of sight, were already returning to the castle, already inventing a historic battle, each engrossed in his own mythology.

Within minutes, television crews were at the gates, filing reports and taking statements from the heroic guards.

A pencil-thin man in a gray suit and wearing television shaped glasses quietly slipped past the gates, as a couple of uniformed police officers tried to corral the cameras. He wondered who had tipped them off, probably the same person who tipped him off. He walked along the perimeter, inspecting the grounds, the wall. He watched the head of security cradling the remains of his dog and whispering the promise of scraps from some heavenly table. He crossed over to the castle, noting the discreet bombs: the homemade charges that had blown the lights. He entered the castle and walked its corridors. He looked about the Diamond Room and up through the hole in the ceiling. He climbed the rope to the roof and slipped out into the moonlight. He turned to where an artificial lake shimmered in the distance, but his vision fell short and he saw only a confusing haze at the limits of his world, limits that he now noticed had been edging ever closer for the past couple of years.

.

02/Death in Repose

Two months earlier, Jack returned from his morning run and collected his mail. He ran up the stairs to his apartment, in order to keep his workout going until he got home. He dropped the post onto the breakfast counter, stretched, and shook the lactic acid from his muscles. He turned the radio on and let the room fill up with power chords. He loved the relentlessness and the bombast of classic rock. A warm shower, a leisurely breakfast, and he felt ready to begin his day. He settled down with a mug of steaming coffee and spread the mail on the table before him. His phone beeped with a text message suggesting lunch.

Jack arrived at the restaurant shortly before one o'clock. Despite having a reservation, he had to wait for a table. From the bar, he had a clear view of the dining room. It was a dark vault filled with what the owners claimed to be a thousand years of Irish history; the timber joists that ran to the center of the ceiling had come from Irish trees. This was the province of a particular type of thief. To Jack, everybody was a thief, but he put himself in a different category to the thieves who ran the restaurant, and the thieves who ate there. He stole from the rich to avoid being poor. They robbed the poor in order to be rich, skimping on quality, or skimming pension funds to pay for their addictions: thousand dollar suits, hookers, and sloops. The exception was Tony, the person Jack was here to meet.

Working as a young thief in the fifties and sixties, Tony loved his life. He felt there was a certain glamor attached to his outlaw status. He was not just a thief, he was sticking it to *The Man*. Because of that image, he was also sticking it to the many daughters of *The Man*. The Future Mothers of America: wholesome looking girls who would prowl college campuses and downtown dive bars, in search of poetry and illicit sex: Indian, Black, Communist or Criminal. They were building memories before the onset of suburban respectability, children and tranquilizers: those magic little pills, which some were already taking from Mother's medicine chest in order to feel rebellious and alive, and which they would one day take in order to feel nothing. One of these women went on to campaign against backward messages on rock albums.

Now an old man, Tony longed to retire, but he had seven ex-wives, twenty-five children, and thirty grandchildren. None of his ex-wives had remarried, five of his children and ten of his grandchildren were in rehab, and all but seven of this little village looked to Tony to support them.

Polite Jazz whispered from loudspeakers as a waiter led Jack to his table. The expression 'Music for Middlebrows' came to mind. He was sipping a glass of water with a couple of lemon and lime wedges floating in it when Tony arrived. He sat down and picked up the menu. As he looked at the prices, the corners of Tony's mouth turned down and with them his whole face seemed to slide a little, as if an avalanche threatened to take hold of his features. He shook his head.

"I remember when you could get a steak sandwich for a buck and a half. It was a good lump of steak too." He put the menu down and looked directly into Jack's eyes. "1.5"

Jack nodded. "1.5."

'1.5' meant one point five million dollars, Jack's fee for

the job he still knew nothing about.

"Good. Let's eat." Their business concluded, the two men ordered lunch and spent half an hour discussing trivialities. There was no talk about the job. Arguably, there was no reason for them to meet, but Tony liked to look into the eyes of the person to whom he assigned a particular job. The occupation notwithstanding, this was the only way he could be sure he was dealing with an honest man.

Jack left the restaurant with a cell phone and a memory stick containing all the information he would need for the job. At home, he plugged the memory stick into his computer and learned he had been hired to steal the Whitely Diamond. He smiled. He had once planned to crown his career by stealing this jewel. But he recognized the vanity of that ambition, the stone would be impossible to sell, and there is no profit in vanity.

In the weeks that followed, Jack made his plans, observing the advice of General Patton: *A good plan, violently executed today, is far better than a perfect plan executed tomorrow.* Jack finished his preparations by taking the night off.

Jack's eyes opened. A little drool fell from the corner of his mouth. He lay twisted across the bed, troubled and still. Dreams of a woman clawed at him and made him afraid. He took a moment to recall where he was. He felt his arm stretch across the empty space beside him. He felt the deeper emptiness of knowing that she was gone. For a few seconds, he thought she was the woman he had dreamed of, and then he remembered: she was a whore, and she was still on the clock. He did not recall her name; he did not recall her leaving, and he was too old for her anyway, even if she was a whore. There was something else, a presence that filled the room.

He found a pair of eyes burning in shadows within shadows as a figure took shape at the foot of the bed. Jack sensed, more than saw, concern cross the face of this phantom. A shift in the atmosphere wiped it all away and left a man, sitting, staring at him, and waiting for him to wake up. He felt the dread of something beyond his control. He felt tightness in his chest, and then a sickness, as if he had just thrown up. He thought he saw a bony finger caress the trigger guard of an automatic pistol – Death in Repose.

Jack's hand began to crawl down the side of the bed.

Death spoke softly, "Don't disturb yourself."

"What's going on?"

"This is just to let you know."

"Know what?"

The figure rose silently in a single movement. Moonlight sparkling on the silver gun in his hand looked like a tiny constellation. Jack followed the movement of these stars until each was extinguished as the intruder reached the bedroom door. Death stopped to look at Jack, and there again came the sense of concern.

"I'm sorry," he said, and slipped quietly out of the room.

As soon as the bedroom door closed, Jack was on his feet. He crossed the room and opened the door. The hallway was empty. He opened the apartment door and walked quickly to the end of the corridor. The elevator was lit up and going down. Jack raced to the stairs, the door was stuck, and he had to put his shoulder to it to get it open. The stairwell was empty. He half ran, half jumped down the concrete steps to the next floor. He came out into the corridor and checked the elevator again. It was two floors below him and still going down. He went back to the stairs and continued running jumping racing the elevator to the ground hardly feeling the cold concrete on his bare feet hoping at least to put a face to the shadow.

He reached the ground floor and stood by the lobby door, his hand on the handle. He took a moment to catch his breath and then softly cracked open the door. The lobby appeared empty. From where he stood, Jack could not see the elevator, but he heard it arrive, he heard the doors open. He knew that anyone leaving the elevator would have to pass him. He waited. No one came. There was silence until he heard the elevator doors close.

"Hello?" the Security Guard's voice echoed in the empty lobby. The clip-clop of his shoes on the marble floor reminded Jack of his own feet turning numb from the cold. He suddenly realized he was naked and blushed at the prospect of running into the old woman who lived in the apartment below him. He closed the door and as quietly as he could, ran up two flights of stairs and out of view. He felt weak. He was aware only of his heart beating and the cold sweat that made him shiver. He continued back up to the seventh floor, keeping an eye out for anyone coming down the stairs.

Jack pushed open his apartment door. The entrance hall was empty. He stepped inside, closed and locked the door. He felt more embarrassed than angry that someone had broken into his home. As a burglar, Jack knew all the vulnerable places in his apartment, and when he first moved in, he made sure to secure them. Until now, his precautions had kept him safe. He pulled on a robe and went out onto the balcony, looking down to the street for anyone coming out of the building. After fifteen minutes with no sightings, Jack went back inside and locked the door. Did his burglar live in the building? Jack had not felt this vulnerable since he was a child growing up in a New York tenement. Even then, the thought that the burglar was probably someone from the neighborhood made it easier to deal with; someone would find them; someone would pay.

Jack turned on all the lights and began to search the apartment, looking for the signs only a professional would recognize. An hour later, he stopped. Half a lifetime's experience had just proved worthless. Jack allowed himself to consider the scarier part of the encounter. Whoever it was had been sitting for however long in the dark, watching him sleep. What was meant by the statement "This is just to let you know." Let him know what? He stopped, arrested by an idea. The whore was in on it. She had let him in. Had she? Was she just some random whore? Was he an assignment? Thoughts of the girl sent him back to the bedroom, but all he found was a burst condom.

All hope of sleep abandoned now, Jack went to the kitchen and put the coffee on, then went through to the living room. He stood for a few moments before one of the bookshelves that lined the apartment, searching for something light. He settled on Ian Fleming's, *Live and Let Die*. He opened the book but found he was unable to concentrate. He decided to try a more challenging book. He did not expect a better result, but the exercise might be useful. He put Fleming away and opened Marcus du Sautoy's *The Music of the Primes*. The book was an adventure in mathematics. It was one of the regrets of Jack's life that he lacked the imagination to appreciate the finer points of mathematics. He could certainly calculate, and he understood that everything aspires to the condition of mathematics. There are those who argue that everything aspires to the condition of music, but what is music without mathematics? A piano keyboard is divided into a repeating pattern of natural, sharp, and flat notes. The scale of C major is C, D, E, F, G, A, B, the final C is actually the beginning of the next round and is played to make the sound complete. In any given scale, the division between each note is always the same, so you can pick any first note, and following this pattern, you will quickly learn the keyboard. The Blues is not a feeling; it is a mathematical construct, man! Unfortunately, though Jack understood the principal, the actual making of music, indeed, the making of any art, escaped him.

Jack had just started to read when all of these thoughts attacked. He put the book aside, turned the television on, and flicked through the news channels. He found a story about a Marine Corps Colonel tracing stolen artifacts. The history of Iraq, worth hundreds of millions of dollars, was being trafficked to London, New York, Paris, and Tokyo. Almost all of it went through Geneva, and frequently it was Iraqis leading the way in selling off their heritage, bringing them more or less into line with the rest of the world. The plunder found its way into the secret vaults of people who told themselves they were preserving the history of this cradle of civilization. Occasionally, customs officers discovered these artifacts in the luggage of ...

Jack changed channels. A new director at the Louvre had removed the Mona Lisa. The exhibit would remain closed for six months to facilitate cleaning and a new study. Angry tourists, in France for this painting alone, complained to their tour operator; they complained again when the tour operator refused to give them a refund. In some quarters, the painting's removal revived speculation that it was a fake. Jack turned the television off. Given the particular news channel, there was no guarantee that the story was accurate, but it would almost certainly become a movie.

Jack showered, dressed and took a shot of espresso. He felt a little better, but there was something he could not escape. He went into the bedroom and found the cell phone Tony had given him. The contact list contained a single number. Jack pressed the call button and as arranged, let the phone ring until it went to voice mail. He left a message, "Hey Tony, it's Jack. How's tricks?" He wanted to know what Tony knew. More importantly, he wanted to know if Tony had sold him out. With fifteen other jobs working, and with everything else Tony had going on, who knew what offers might start to look attractive. Although risks were an accepted part of the job, Jack did not intend to walk into a killing zone.

Half an hour at the meeting point with no sign of Tony. In a situation like this, Tony was always prompt. His absence, coupled with the break-in, told Jack that everything was wrong. At best, something had happened to Tony, but killing him made no sense, he always worked through the client's agent. The thief never met anyone except Tony; the client was always protected.

Jack crossed the city and changed cars, then crossed the city again to what he hoped was still his safe house. He took the elevator to the top floor.

The sun made mirrors of the city, and the apartment was stifling. Jack opened all the windows to let in as much air as possible before the rush hour arrived, spewing out noise and smoke and forcing him to shut it out and turn the air conditioning on. He paced the floor, trying to decide what to do next.

03/Aftermath of the Robbery

After escaping the Whitely Museum, Jack walked quickly past the chaos on the freeway, to the rest stop where his car sat waiting. He opened the door and suddenly laughed, realizing the storm had cleared as soon as he had cleared the castle grounds. He sat into the car and turned the key in the ignition. It had been serviced in preparation for tonight's job and so should have started first time, but it wheezed, coughed and almost stalled. Jack had a vision of a police car pulling up, some rookie cop coming over to see what the problem was, and arresting him just to be on the safe side. The car finally sputtered into life, and Jack was able to breathe again. He let the engine turn over a few times before taking his place in the stream: another anonymous family car headed out of town. A station wagon cruised past, trailing a fantasy: aluminum siding, barbecues, basketball hoops, grazed knees and soda pops, white picket fences. Jack had no idea what that would really mean, but at that moment, PTA meetings, dental appointments, arguments over wallpaper, or more precisely, his lack of interest in wallpaper, all of these things held an almost exotic fascination for him. Once upon a time, he told a woman that so long as she did not turn their house into a Barbie dream home, he did not care what it looked like. That was the last time Jack made domestic arrangements with anyone.

Coming down from the high of the job, hunger filled Jack's stomach. He picked a gas-station sandwich from the passenger seat and ripped the plastic covering with his teeth. He gagged as his head jerked away from the stink of stale cheese and rotten ham.

A car horn shocked his mind into focus. He was riding the white line, headlights flashed in his rear-view mirror. He eased back into his own lane, watching an angry finger in a passing window. All of this happened in less time than it takes to describe. Jack rolled the window down. He took a moment to catch his breath and then, without stopping or slowing, and trying to keep an eye on the road, he reached across to roll down the passenger side window. The car began to swerve. There was a sudden noise. A motorcycle tore past, Morse code obscenities blasting from the horn. Jack felt his hands shaking on the wheel. Doubt began to overtake him. He moved into the fast lane, trying to outrun everything until the cars thinned out, and he was cruising comfortably along the open road. He turned the radio on and recognized the sound of Bon Jovi. He turned it off. Poodle haircuts and Rock 'N' Roll just do not work.

Twenty miles out of town, Jack pulled in at a gas station. He got out of the car, stretched, yawned, and filled the tank. As he walked to the store to pay, he noticed a Highway Patrol motorcycle parked around the side of the building. Jack opened the door, stepped into harsh strip lighting and the sweet sound of a light voice singing heavy songs. A cop stood talking to the kid behind the counter. They watched Jack as he went to the chilled cabinet and picked up a corned beef sandwich and a soda, taking extra care to check the date on both. After paying, he took his food over to a seated area.

He recognized the music; the voice belonged to Harriet Wheeler – English Indie Totty – it was The Sundays' debut album: *reading, writing and arithmetic*. Jack sat happily eating his food and remembering a girl from years ago who let him fantasize that he was having sex with Harriet Wheeler. The girl did not know she was doing this.

The cop sauntered over and began to chat about the

mess on the freeway. When the cop asked his destination, Jack answered with the cover Tony had set up for him. He was on his way to Lake George for a weekend with the guys. Thankful for the distraction, he could slip into character and escape the mistakes he had made tonight. The cop was also thankful: his stretch of highway was quiet and cold, and he spent most of his shift drinking coffee and wasting time with the kid who worked at the gas station.

Jack finished his sandwich, said goodbye to the cop and got up to leave. As he opened the shop door, Jack noticed a copy of *Perfect Strangers*, Deep Purple's comeback album. He bought the LP when it first came out but had not listened to it in years. Seeing it now made him wonder why he had never bought a copy for the car. If anyone ever made great driving music, it was Deep Purple. He picked up the CD and waved it at the cop.

"You remember this?"

"No, man. I was four years old."

"Showing my age." Jack laughed. He took the CD to the cash register. The kid behind the counter gave him a funny *Dad Rock* look, he had heard of Deep Purple, but he had never heard them.

Feeling warm inside, Jack returned to his car and got in. He put the CD into the player, pushed play and headed out onto the freeway. A few miles further on Jack picked up a steak, beer and fries at a convenience store, then continued on his way. He drove until his was the only car on the road, by which time he had passed two motels. The letters TV blinked red in the sky. Drawing closer, he saw the dilapidated sign OTEL. He pulled into a vast courtyard overlooked by two floors of anonymity.

The Manager, a snaggle-tooth wreck of a man, turned away from the television and, his right hand feeling for the shotgun under the counter, looked with suspicion at the stranger who entered the office.

Jack nodded. "I almost missed you," he said.

"Yeah?" The Manager waited a moment for Jack to speak, and then asked, "You need a room?"

"Yeah."

"Rates up there. Pay in advance." He jerked his thumb towards a price list framed in gold: someone's idea of refinement. A room cost twenty dollars an hour, fifty dollars for the night. Jack paid for the night. The manager pushed a registration card over to him and after Jack had filled it out, slammed a key down on the counter. At precisely the same moment, a cartoon shotgun blast turned each man's head towards the TV. The Manager sniggered. He fingered the key a little closer to Jack.

"Room fourteen. Second floor. On the end."

Jack said "Thanks," but the manager had already returned to the epic story of humanity's insignificance in the face of nature: Bugs Bunny walking along behind a blissfully ignorant Elmer Fudd. Jack left the office; he collected his overnight bag from the car and walked to his room.

Climbing the steps to the second floor, he caught a few bars of Waylon Jennings singing *Mammas, Don't Let Your Babies Grow Up To Be Cowboys*. As Jack approached room fourteen, the song grew louder, and he found himself singing along, *"They'll never stay home, and they're always alone, even with someone they love.*

Jack let himself into his room. He dropped his things on the bed, then locked the door and wedged a chair under the handle.

Waylon finished his set and then came what Jack supposed to be the headline act. It sounded like a drill. After a few revs, the sound changed, became deeper, providing a backing track for squeals of pain turning to pleasure, followed moments later by the percussive grunts of a determined savage.

The motel was Tony's protocol; otherwise Jack would have gone home. "You never know who's watching you, so go to a motel until the job's done." That would not be until Jack handed over the diamond. For now he needed somewhere to hide it. He went into the bathroom, for a moment he considered dropping the diamond into the toilet, after dinner, but he might flush it down in the morning. He opened the bathroom window and looked out. The back of the motel was in darkness, save for the overspill of light from the occupied rooms. A few old carports stood apparently empty, beyond them, neat rows of naked trees filed away to darkness. Where to hide the diamond? He closed the window and went back into the main room. At a small kitchen area, Jack prepared his dinner of steak and french fries. When his food was ready, he emptied it onto a plate and found the perfect hiding place for the diamond. He dropped it into the grease that had just fried his frenchies, watched it sink and turn invisible. He opened a bottle of Guinness Extra Stout, found a news channel on the television, and sat down to dinner.

The news reported that a burglar had breached the state-of-the-art security system at the Whitely Museum and stolen the Whitely Diamond. Celebrity Experts discussed the logistics of how the burglary might have been committed, the equipment the thief must have used, and where one could buy these things. From the police briefing, the news crews learned that the burglar had entered through the roof. There were boot prints in the grass. These slender facts inspired discussions about how fit the burglar must have been; a personal trainer came on to demonstrate the exercise regime needed to maintain that level of fitness. News of the boot print led to a history of footwear in crime. An online psychologist came on to discuss his theory that ill-fitting shoes create ill-fitting people, this is what gives rise to crime. Also from the boot print, one enterprising reporter extrapolated an entire wardrobe. Exactly what should one wear to commit a burglary in winter?

Jack finished his dinner and turned the television off.

Back when he had friends, this was the kind of story they loved: human interest, as told by people whose only interest in humans is how to exploit them. He turned the lights off and sat on the bed.

Morning came sweetly, fresh and clear, creeping in under the door and making the curtains glow bright orange on the window. Sunlight brought silence, blessed, forgiving silence, to the room next-door. Several times during the night, Jack wanted to turn the TV on, just to mask the sound of the equestrian show in room thirteen. But he was afraid to do anything that might give him away.

From four blocks away, Jack felt the pull of the church. Candlelight played on the translucent white face of Mary. Shrouded by shadow in the marble folds of Her dress was the life that Jack had lost. He drew a long thin candle from the box, lit it off someone else's prayer, and fixed it to a holder. Kneeling at Her feet, Jack tried to pray. His mouth formed words that fell soundlessly to the floor, and if anything was reaching for him, he was beyond it. He shifted uncomfortably and caught the attention of a couple passing. They turned towards him and saw what appeared to be an old man out of time. They could sense the space around him. They caught his eye and then quickly turned towards their own devotion. They would pray for him, but he was not one of them.

Jack stood up and looked at the people scattered among the pews. To his surprise, there were as many young people as there were old. He pictured himself as one of them, enrobed in faith and connected to ... whatever it was. Someone coughed, and the image melted away to reality, it simply did not fit. Jack could light candles and offer up his words, but he remained unmoved. When you die, you decompose – end of story. Despite knowing this, he knew he would keep coming back. He left the church. There was a chill in the air, and he turned up the collar of his sports coat. He put his hands in his pockets and felt something hard wrapped in paper. He had forgotten about the diamond. He began to think about the handover. Then, up the road, he noticed a girl selling flags for a local anti-poverty organization. He stood watching her, watching people pass by without giving. He smiled, recalling one of his Grandfather's sayings: 'God is a pure Divil, when he wants to be.'

Jack had come out of the church intending to fully discharge his contract. Now, seeing this girl, her youth, his own encroaching middle age... Although not generally given to sentiment, he found himself weighing the girl against *The Fat Man*. Jack always thought of the client as *The Fat Man*. He pictured some *Sidney Greenstreet*, swollen with avarice and empire, clammy hands that closed around the world like damp paper. He thought of the bargain he had struck, the one point five million dollars he had been paid to steal the diamond. He thought about Tony, what had become of him? Would he be there to take possession? To hell with it, the strict terms of the contract were to steal the Whitely Diamond and to leave irrefutable proof of the theft. Well, he had stolen the diamond. He had left irrefutable proof of the theft. It was on the news. Weighing the girl against all of that, Jack decided he had fulfilled his contract. That he now chose to give the diamond to someone else was his own business. *The Fat Man* could take the hit.

As Jack approached the girl, nervous fingers played with the diamond in his pocket. To quell his doubts he invented a life of grinding poverty, from which this diamond, and only this diamond, would release her. He knew the argument was nonsense, but the stone was insured for twenty million dollars, and the company would pay ten percent for recovery.

From the corner of his eye, Jack saw her smile, broad and generous, easy. There was not the relentless pursuit of a commission that so many of these people try to hide behind a friendly facade.

It was refreshing to find nothing practiced about this girl. She was exactly as he pictured her. She could be his daughter. Without breaking his stride as he passed, Jack dropped the diamond into her bucket.

04/Masterson

In a riot of orange and yellow, the sun rose above a dirt track that cut its way through a tangled forest, where all the unknown dangers of the world lay waiting. Beyond this, a vast savannah stretched to the horizon.

Every time he entered his apartment, this painting captured Jack. He could feel the colors calling, the light spilling out from the painting, the yellows and greens, the soft blue sky streaked with orange, revived him as it woke up the world. He stood before this promise of redemption, letting it break the spell of his occupation and allow him to feel human again. After a moment, he took off his jacket and opened the living room door.

"Jack." An oversized old man on the couch looked up from a book in his lap. His voice was as expansive as his waist, and a thin smile stretched across a face that showed no other sign of emotion.

Jack pulled the door shut. A hand gripped the back of his neck. He walked quickly backward, forcing the man behind him up against the wall. He hammered his right elbow into soft flesh and stepped away. He turned. A short round man, clutching his stomach, folded to the floor.

As Jack reached for the front door, a single word stopped him.

"No." It was the voice of his mysterious burglar. Jack released the door latch at the sound of a hammer being pulled back. He raised his hands.

"Turn around."

Jack turned to find the burglar standing by the bedroom door. The eyes that had burned in darkness, in daylight seemed to hold an odd mix of intelligence and sorrow. Only the gun was unaltered. He motioned Jack towards the living room door. The fat man raised his hand. "Wait a minute." He stood up, holding onto the wall. He took a small brush from his pocket and began dusting himself down. When he finished with his clothes, he used the same brush to tidy his hair. While he did this, his companion thumbed the hammer of his gun; he had seen it all before. After making himself presentable, the fat man put the brush back in his pocket. He went over to Jack and slapped him across the face. Again. Again.

"OK, that's enough," the gunman said.

The fat man slapped Jack again.

"Enough!"

The fat man turned with venom, ready to strike. He stopped when he saw the gun. The other man jerked the gun towards the living-room door. The fat man took a step, then turned and backhanded Jack across the face.

"You can play with him later," the gunman said.

The fat man opened the living room door and entered. Jack followed and once again received the warm greeting: "Jack. So, you're a poet. I don't think I've ever met anybody who uses Larkin as a coffee table book. Did your Mum and Dad fuck you up?" The old man smiled; he put the book aside and looked about the room, making a show of taking in the furniture. His disapproval, and even sadness, was genuine. All Jack required of his furniture was that it do its job. Chairs were for sitting on, and so, when he came to furnish the apartment, Jack went to an outlet store and bought the cheapest, sturdiest things they had.

"I would have expected a man like you to have better taste than this, Jack."

Everything about the old man was large. He was a caricature villain from the worst kind of pulp: henna black hair piled high on his head, his eyebrows, dyed the same color as his hair, looked glued in place. He appeared to be wearing make-up, and then Jack realized the unnaturally smooth skin was the effect of Botox: poison injected into the face to create the illusion of youth. An Armani suit struggled to contain his bulk. He stripped his porcelain teeth in what he supposed was a smile. Intended to complete the illusion of youth, the teeth succeeded only in adding years to the face from which they beamed so unnaturally white. Jack laughed; it occurred to him that American dentistry would one day be visible from space. He moved just in time to escape a punch. He swung his elbow up, making contact with the fat man's face. As Jack turned, the butt of the gun slammed down on the back of his neck. He fell to his knees. The old man waved a hand, and Jack was placed in a chair. The two others retreated to the door.

"It's OK Jack," the old man was almost paternal, "we're not here to harm you. Despite..." He gestured towards the door.

"Then what do you want?"

"It's a question of values, Jack." He paused, and there was something practiced about it, as if he had gone over this scene hundreds of times, practicing each moment, weighing each word until all appeared spontaneous. "You don't have any," he said. "I don't mean family values, Jack; I mean real values, the values that come from a solid moral center.

"You have no moral center, Jack. That slip of a girl the other night." He smiled again, but there was fury in his eyes. They spoke of this and other things and then the old man said, "You have spent your life without any real values. Now, you may argue that you only steal from those who can afford to take the hit, and some of them can. Some of them can afford to take the hit better than ninety-nine percent of the population. But the question, Jack, the question is this: do they take the hit?" He paused, apparently waiting for an answer. He made a steeple of his fingertips, closed his eyes a moment and smiled before continuing. "The answer, Jack, is no. No. They do not take the hit. They do not take the hit because they are in a position to pass it on to people lower down in the food chain.

"They pass it on to garbage men, to schoolteachers, to kids trying to buy their first home. The people that suffer, Jack, are the same people that always suffer. The people who ultimately pay for your crimes are the people who can least afford it.

"And then there are those who cannot afford to take the hit, those who can't pass it on. Five years ago you robbed a man called Bill Clinton, an unfortunate name. Bill Clinton was living hand-to-mouth, on a higher plateau, to be sure, but still ... As a direct result of your action, he lost everything; he hanged himself two weeks later. Those are some of the consequences of your life."

These were ideas that had never occurred to Jack. He listened to them now without emotion.

"We've left you alone until now because, until recently, you've been outside of our jurisdiction. Your next job, however, will be within our jurisdiction." Again the old man paused, and waited for Jack to answer, and again Jack sat sullenly staring back at him. The old man raised his fingers like some pontiff granting a special dispensation.

"I have it within my power to legitimize your assets."

Now, for the first time, Jack's face betrayed his interest. The old man picked up a small attaché case. Without taking his eyes off Jack, he reached into the case and withdrew the Whitely Diamond. He held it out to Jack.

"Did you honestly believe that, in this day and age, you could anonymously dispose of such a famous stone?"

The old man threw down a security camera photograph of Jack dropping the diamond into the anti-poverty bucket.

"Did you think you were saving yourself? Listen to me, Jack. This is the truth that sets you free: you have what you commit yourself to having, you live as you commit yourself to living, you are who you commit yourself to being.

"But know this: there is nowhere you can go that we will not see you. There is no conversation you can have that we will not overhear. There is nothing you can do that we cannot stop you if we choose." Another pause. "You did a good thing here Jack, and because of you, that girl will now get to go to college. I thought that was very human. That is why I have decided to give you a chance."

The old man put the jewel on the table, and from the attaché case, he now drew a five-pound hammer and a cloth. He covered the diamond and brought the hammer down hard on top of it. A loud crash filled the room, and bits of glass flew out from beneath. The old man sat back. Jack waited. He knew what was expected: raise the cloth, complete the trick. Jack did not believe in magic, but he played his part, lifting the cloth to reveal the shattered remains of the Whitely Diamond spread out around a ring of ground glass in the veneer.

"There is no Whitely Diamond, Jack. There never was."

In the early nineteenth century, the first George Whitely built his fortune on the reality of this diamond. He had learned his craft sitting on his father's knee, "A fool and his money are easily parted. Spin a good yarn and everyone's a fool."

Whitely learned the trade of diamond cutting and quickly built a reputation for the quality of his work and of his character. When he announced his intention of going to Africa to look for diamonds, he became a hero to the staid world of his clients. Soon after his departure, stories began to arrive, and those stories became the Whitely Diamond. Before anyone had set eyes on it, the Whitely Diamond was legendary.

On his return from Africa, Whitely borrowed against

the diamond and bought shares in munitions companies: the bullets and guns that would civilize the nation. He invested in companies making covered wagons, shovels, picks and pans, and all the paraphernalia of gold fever. He then infected a few carefully chosen people with this sickness. Within six months, he had tripled his money, within a year he was one of the richest people he knew, and still no gold had been found. Some looked down on him as *new money*, but as his supporters pointed out, all wealthy families were once *Nouveau Riche*, and *old money* usually means that a criminal past has been forgotten or excused.

Doubts about the authenticity of the diamond were ignored, and the diamond itself obscured by stories of savage tribes, and by the growing bank accounts of his backers.

His talent allowed the hustler to marry into the upper echelons of Boston society and realize the dream of generations by becoming a *toff*, although he never forgot what *those people* really were.

Jack looked at the old man who sat quietly waiting, like someone certain of getting what he wanted.

"CIA?"

"No, Jack. The CIA is a terror organization. The CIA overthrows democracies and installs dictators, the CIA trains terrorists, the CIA kidnap people and send them overseas to be tortured. I do not work for the CIA. As I said, I have it within my power to legitimize your assets: if you do a job for us."

Jack smiled. "There's always a catch."

The old man motioned to the others to leave the room. When they had gone, Jack and the old man sat looking at each other for several seconds before Jack began to rise out of his chair. The old man reached for something inside his jacket. Jack paused, "I need a drink."

The old man nodded.

"Do you want one?" Jack asked.

"No. Tell me Jack, what do you know about the Mona Lisa?"

"It's a painting."

A tense silence filled the room as the old man tried to decide if Jack was laughing at him. He let it go.

"Yes. It is a painting. Mona Lisa. La Giaconda. Her name was Lisa Gherardini. Married to a Florentine businessman, one Francesco del Giaconda. DaVinci spent four years working on the painting. He brought it with him everywhere.

"On the 21 August 1911 a certain Vincenzo Peruggia stole it. He worked at the Louvre and one day, after work, he hid in a closet until the museum closed. When everybody had gone home, he, OK, he came out of the closet, he took the painting down from the wall and walked out of the building, his lady hidden under his coat.

"He was working for a man called Eduardo de Valfierno. Unknown to Peruggia, long before the theft, de Valfierno commissioned copies of the painting, and these were already safely overseas, with buyers waiting, each one believing that he was going to buy the original. De Valfierno left Peruggia hanging. Two years later, Peruggia decided he'd had enough. He was caught trying to sell the painting. Officially, it was returned to the Louvre in 1913."

"Unofficially?"

"Unofficially, it is believed the original was never recovered, and it is one of the copies that now draw the crowds.

"An underground organization in Paris claim to have the original. They're putting it up for sale. I want you to find out if it's real. If it is, I want you to bid for it."

As he looked at the old man, Jack realized that he had not given his name. "If I'm going to be working for you, what's your name?"

"Masterson."

"And who do you work for?"

An Empire of Silence

"You don't need to know that." Masterson rested his right elbow on the arm of the couch. He touched his thumb to his chin and his forefinger to his temple, a position he believed gave him the appearance of an intellectual. The sleeve of his jacket fell down a little, revealing a microphone, the sort of thing Secret Service men have hidden in their sleeves. Jack's laugh met with fury in Masterson's eyes. He snapped his fingers. The door opened, and the two men returned. They stood awaiting orders. With them came the memory of pain to Jack's body. He looked at the whisky bottle. He thought of the damage he could do.

"I need an answer now, Jack."

"You'll pay my expenses?"

Masterson pulled a plane ticket from his attaché case. He moved the whisky bottle out of Jack's reach and replaced it with the ticket. "That's a First Class ticket to London."

"You said Paris."

"I said an underground organization in Paris has the painting. Nobody knows where the sale will take place. London is the meeting point. We've booked a suite in your name at the Dorchester." For a moment, something approaching pride showed in his eyes. "The same suite President Eisenhower stayed in when he was Supreme Commander of the Allied Forces during World War Two."

Jack, confident that every suite was the same suite President Eisenhower stayed in, was unimpressed. "So, I get to London, then what?"

"Someone will contact you."

"How did you find out about this sale?"

"Yes or No, Jack. Will you take the job?"

Jack turned to the men by the door; they stood impassive, staring at him. Together they gave the impression of a malicious Laurel and Hardy. At a push, Jack felt he could take one of them, but he might also take a bullet to the head. He turned back to Masterson. "Do I have a choice?"

"Ah." The corners of Masterson's lips curled up into two little fishhooks. "Democracy in Action," he said. His eyes shone, dark and beautiful; his face became animated and seemed to offer friendship. "You always have a choice."

"I have a question," Jack said.

"Of course."

"What happens if I get the painting for you and it turns out to be a forgery?"

"No, no, no." Masterson's finger moved like a metronome. "You are not to buy the painting. You are to find out if it is real, and if so, you are to bid, not buy."

"I want all my assets legitimized before I leave."

Masterson took a long white envelope from an inside pocket of his jacket. "You leave tomorrow. Obviously, for all your assets to be legitimized, they would need to be listed. I have been authorized to do that. This," he shook the envelope, "is not that authorization. This is your arrest warrant. Do the job. Come home. You're a free man." He threw the envelope down on the table; Jack picked it up and opened it. He withdrew the warrant, looked it over and smiled.

"OK," said Jack, "you've got yourself a thief."

"No, Jack. You are now in a world of truth. You bid. That's all. Money is no object. You bid. Regardless of the price.

"It will come down to you and one other man. He will buy the painting; he has unlimited resources, so you bid. Drive the price up. The man we want is his boss. You bid. That's all."

"Fair enough." Jack did not believe a word of this, but lights were coming on across the city, and the morning may depend on him taking the job.

"Excellent. Clarence will pick you up in the morning and take you to the airport."

Jack turned to the men by the door. "Which one is

Clarence?"

Neither man gave any indication that this name belonged to him, so Jack added, "The fat guy?"

A flash of anger came to the fat man's eyes, his jaw tensed, but he held his place.

"No," said Masterson, "that is not Clarence."

When he was alone, Jack relaxed into the bouquet of good whisky. After the drink, he took a long hot shower which he finished by turning the water to cold, shocking the blood to his skin, waking up all his senses. He wrapped himself in a thick Turkish towel and went through to the living room. Looking across the city towards the airport, he wondered how he was going to get on that plane tomorrow. He hated flying. The idea that a monstrous machine could be carried along at hundreds of miles per hour, thousands of feet in the air, seemed ludicrous. Although he knew the statistics supported a safe journey, another part of him wondered what would support the plane in flight if any one of a thousand things went wrong.

05/Culture

Jack sat up in bed, struggling to identify what had startled him from sleep.

Two gunshots sounded, and a gruff voice called for somebody named MacKay to "Come on out here." It was a western on television. Jack got out of bed, and then remembered he had not been watching television the night before. As he reached the bedroom door, he realized it was Clarence, come to take him to the airport. He sat on the bed and listened to the gunfight. He found himself entertaining the question of murder. His thoughts filled him with a sense of loathing he had never known before. As sure as he was that Clarence was a psychopath, Jack was equally certain there were people who loved him, simply because they did. Would his murder lessen or increase their pain? Would it make Jack's world any more secure? He rubbed his eyes and scratched himself; it was too early in the morning for questions of morality. Perhaps, when the job was finished, he would be free.

Jack pulled on a robe and went to the kitchen. He stopped at the door, suddenly blinded by sunlight bouncing off the brushed steel and white tile. His eyes closed, and his head turned away. He was still half-asleep and had to lean against the doorjamb for support. The smell of fresh coffee. He went to the window and pulled the blind down, returning the room to its natural state. He poured a mug of coffee and raised it to his lips, breathing in the aroma before that first bitter sip. A noise from the living room. Jack thought again of the day that was ahead. He opened the refrigerator door in search of food but found only an empty vodka bottle. Again, the thought of murder crossed Jack's mind. Swearing, he slammed the refrigerator door closed and went to the living room.

Clarence, stretched out on the couch, had his feet up on the table, a bowl of cereal in his lap. Jack surveyed the scene. An automatic pistol sat with the sugar bowl and the empty milk bottle by the feet dressed in patent-leather shoes. A glass tumbler with a little water in it on the other side of the table.

"I threw your food out so it doesn't go to waste," Clarence said. "It's a sin to waste food."

"Do you always begin your day with a drink?" Jack asked.

"Never touch the stuff."

Seeing Clarence watching television, with a library on three sides, Jack's mind began to calculate his chances.

Clarence looked at the gun. "My cold companion," he said. "Give it a try." He turned his attention back to the television. He shoveled another spoonful of Sugar Puffs into his mouth, and then burst out laughing at the movie.

"How did you get in?" Jack asked.

"Boss has a master key."

"I had a chain on the door."

Clarence looked up at Jack, then down at the gun. He reached across to the sugar, filled his spoon, and poured it over the cereal. He continued to eat.

Jack began to feel weak, his strength suddenly drained. He stood there, hopeless, useless. Vacantly he scanned the spines of his books for help but found none. He turned to anger, and the pitiful solace of a single, powerful kick to the backs of Clarence's legs. With the kick, Clarence's knees jerked sharply up, throwing honeyed milk and cereal over his shirt front and his chin. There was a beat in which time was suspended and then, slowly, Clarence turned, confused as to why Jack would risk everything for, well, for nothing. The two men held each other's gaze, tense and waiting, vying for dominance, for any edge that might help them in battle. Then Clarence swung the bowl in a wide arc and let it fly. Jack moved just enough to escape the worst of it. The bowl clipped his shoulder. Clarence grabbed his gun and lashed out as he stood up. His forearm crashed into Jack's throat. He stumbled backward, choking. Clarence swung round and kicked Jack's legs out from under him. As Jack hit the ground, he found Clarence on top of him, pushing the gun into his face. Every impulse told Clarence to kill, but he was under orders. His gun hand jerked. Not knowing what to do, Clarence forced the gun barrel between Jack's lips. Confusion in the killer's eyes relieved Jack's fear, and his own eyes smiled back, perhaps his rebellion had not been so pathetic, after all. Ordinarily, a show of disrespect like that would have meant death, but for all the power he invested in his *cold companion*, Clarence himself had none. He released Jack and stood up, looking disgusted at his shirtfront. He wiped himself down as best he could and watched Jack get up off the floor.

"Get yourself cleaned up," Clarence ordered. He looked at the gun in his hand as if he no longer understood its purpose. "Your bags are over there."

He holstered the gun under his left arm and buttoned his jacket. For the first time in years, Clarence was aware of the bulge, like a growth on his side. He could feel the weight of it, the shape of it pressing into him, and it made him feel like James Bond.

Clarence was proud of his employment record. Ten years of murder allowed him to hold his head high when he went home at the end of the day. A pillar of the community, he resented the fact that his tax dollars helped to support welfare scum. From time to time, after an argument with his wife, Clarence would take his rage out on one of these worthless bums.

Usually, Clarence would pick a woman in her twenties and take her to his soundproofed rumpus room. He would wine her, dine her and break her bones, enjoy her screams, shoot her in the belly and rape the bitch until tranquility returned, and life no longer bothered him. Then he'd put a bullet in her brain, tidy up, take a shower, climb the stairs to the family home and wrap himself in the warmth of the people he loved. Stepping lightly through the house so as not to disturb his son, Clarence would slide into bed beside his wife. She would turn to him and apologize for the argument; he would apologize for the argument. They would kiss and cuddle and have make-up sex and sleep, entwined in each other's forgiveness, happy and at peace with themselves and each other.

Fear rode the elevator down with Jack. Clarence, standing behind, hummed softly as he watched the numbers change. The doors opened at the garage. Jack took a step; Clarence put a hand on his arm, "Wait." He stepped out first and looked around. Long practiced in paranoia, he was not about to let anything happen to the most significant package of his career. When he was sure they were alone, he nodded to Jack to follow.

Jack stepped out of the elevator; the doors closed and the security camera took a photograph of both men.

Walking to the car, the only sound was their echoing footsteps. Clarence unlocked the driver side door and sat into his red VW bug. He kissed two fingers and touched them to the feet of Christ crucified on the dashboard. Now he could close the door and pop the trunk for Jack to throw his bags in. When Jack closed the trunk, he saw Clarence kiss a photograph and lean across the dashboard.

Jack sat into the car and saw a small family portrait fixed beneath the cross: Clarence towering over a young, pretty woman and child whose smiles were a little too fixed, their eyes a little too wide open, distorting their faces, and adding an air of tragedy to what should have been an ordinary family picnic. Jack noticed a small brown splatter on the photograph. It took a moment for him to realize the stain was dried blood. Suddenly he had an image of Clarence beating someone to death, then getting into his car and performing his ritual: bloody hands caressing his wife and child. This family car was a hearse with a child seat. Jack imagined the child dropping his toy, the toy picking up the blood, the child picking up the toy and putting it into his mouth, consuming the remains of his father's victims.

Sitting in his family car, Clarence seemed like a different man, the anger was gone, or at least hidden from view. When they were on the road, he began to speak, talking as if they were old friends.

"Have you been to London before?"

"No," Jack said.

"Me neither. I saw Cats. The show. That was written by an English guy. Andrew Lloyd-Webber. When I was courting. She took me to it. She waited a year to get tickets. Said I needed some culture. On Broadway. It was like when I was a kid. I grew up in Jersey. Every summer, when other people were going to Florida, we'd go into Manhattan and see shows. *Annie Get Your Gun*, *On The Town*, things like that. You know Kirk Douglas was cast in the original Broadway production of *On The Town*, you seen the movie?"

"Yeah."

"Well, Kirk Douglas was cast in the Gene Kelly role. But he got laryngitis. And he's a fuckin' Jew. You believe that? What kind of Jew pussies out of a chance to make all that money."

His face relaxed as a sudden thought took hold. "Maybe that's what Hitler meant."

"What?"

"Hitler said everybody knows one good Jew, right? Maybe he was talking about Kirk Douglas. Maybe Kirk Douglas is a good Jew. Anyway, my old lady got the idea that English musical theater is better than American musical theater, so she took me to see Cats."

"Any good?"

"Buncha pussies dressed as cats," he continued without a hint of irony. "American musical theater is the best in the world. Look at that movie, The Phantom of the Opera."

"That's Lloyd-Webber as well, isn't it?"

"It's American money. And that girl, Emmy Rossum."

"I thought she was a Canadian child star."

"No man, New York City. And she's old enough to bleed. That's what counts. Anyway, Canadians are just embarrassed Americans."

Jack had an impulse to reach across and smash Clarence's head down on the steering wheel, but whatever his private feelings, for the moment there was no escaping. They would soon be at the airport, and he could get away.

"I thought about becoming an actor." For a moment, Clarence burned with the flame of his early ambition. Then he was back in the car, a reliable family man. "When I was a kid. A proper actor. Like Brando. Schwarzenegger. That man knows how to act." He paused, "Schwarzenegger. Sounds like a Saturday night in Texas: 'Let's get likkered up an' go Schwarz a *Nigger!*'" He laughed at the brilliance of his humor. He pictured himself on stage at Madison Square Garden with Andrew Dice Clay, the greatest American comedian since Bob Hope. "Good actor, Schwarzenegger. You see *Jingle All The Way*? They don't make 'em like that anymore."

Jack coughed to stifle a laugh when he realized Clarence was being serious.

"You know what would be a cool movie for him?"

"Who?" Jack asked.

"Schwarzenegger."

"What?"

"The Gambler."

"Dostoevsky?"

"Who? No, fuck. Kenny Rogers!"

Clarence turned a sour face on Jack and shook his head, then looked back to the road and concentrated on his driving. In his heart, he despaired at the lack of culture among the criminal classes.

"Anyway," Clarence continued, "I was going to be an actor. I was going to school and everything. Then she got pregnant. So..." In his mind, these two events were inextricably bound together; in reality they were years apart. Clarence paused in remembrance of his lost hopes: the young man auditioning for a place at the American Academy of Dramatic Arts. The year of frustration, the anger that brought him to murder and the murder that brought him peace. In reality, he felt nothing when he killed. He recalled his decision that he had a talent for murder, and his later decision that this could be a career.

When Clarence started talking again, it was with the voice of someone who knows exactly who to blame for all of his mistakes.

"Immigrants get all the good parts anyway. Looka that guy, Jean-Claude Van Damme. Son of a..." Clarence stopped, confused, he was thinking about Mother Van Damme, just because her son was a cunt, did not make her a bitch. He continued, "Anyway, I already had this job. I wasn't about to give up that security. Not in today's world. Not with a kid on the way. You got any kids?"

"No."

"Everyone should have a kid. They really put things in perspective. I know a guy can get you one cheap. Expensive to bring up though. We pay four grand a month childcare. He says he wants to be an Astronaut. So I gotta work, so there's money for him to go to college."

"Not many holidays then?"

"We gotta place in Florida; go down there in the summer. Melbourne, full of old people, nobody bothers us, and I can get away from all this."

He seemed to have finished, and Jack began to feel uncomfortable. "I thought Miami was the place to be?" he asked.

Clarence thought about this. He had a vision of Miami in the nineteen fifties: a colorful world in black and white.

"Miami used to be good, in the old days. That's what I hear." He saw Cubans wash up on South Beach. His head shook like he was having a spasm. The car pulled to the left. The blast of a horn.

"Fuck you," Clarence shouted. Then, almost to himself, "Miami ... just niggers and queers now ... all over the fuckin' place."

His knuckles were white on the wheel.

"So what are you going to do?"

"Like I said, we gotta place down there. Soon as I have the money, I'm gonna retire. I'm gonna start a little theater. Musical theater. For kids. So they got something to do. So they don't end up dealing drugs. Give them some self-respect. They can go out. Get a job. Make the big bucks. Provide for their family. Like me. Every job I do is money in the bank, food on the table

"If I had to, I could lay my hands on two million dollars. All earned."

"Me too," Jack said.

Clarence's eyes shot across to the cunt beside him, then turned to the dashboard shrine for help, but found none. He looked back to the road and focused on his driving. His fingers tightened on the steering wheel. The traffic was moving too damn slow. Clarence slammed his hand down on the horn and tried to pull out to overtake the line of cars in front. At every failed attempt, he mumbled some sort of damnation on the fuckers. They drove like this for a couple of blocks before his bile forced Clarence to speak.

"Don't ever compare yourself to me." The words were a growl that might have gone unnoticed if not for the hate in his voice. Jack turned. Clarence was ready to stop the car, and for a moment, Jack thought his blood might be added to the stains at the picnic.

"You steal things that other people have earned."

Clarence spoke at the car in front. "That is not a profession. Sneaking around stealing things that other people have worked for is not a profession. You're a thief. I work for a living. You're lower than the scum on welfare. I have earned every cent I've ever had in my life. You are a thief. That's not man's work."

"And what you do is?"

"You're damn right it is," Clarence snapped. "It's what this country was built on."

He tightened his grip on the steering wheel and felt the pain in his hands. His jaw set a little harder. The conversation was over. Jack had questioned Clarence's integrity, and someone would pay for the sting. They continued in silence until Clarence pulled into the short stay car park at Logan Airport. Jack opened the car door.

"Wait a minute." Clarence let out heavy breath. He released the trunk. "Get your bags. I have to make sure you get on the plane." They walked together to terminal E and went in, Clarence sticking to Jack until he had gone through to the departure lounge.

Jack strapped himself into his seat and hoped for the best. Added to his usual nervousness about flying was his recent discovery that since the smoking ban on aircraft, incidents of air-rage had increased. Airlines saved money by not cleaning the air properly. Watching the theater of the safety demonstration, Jack recalled an old joke, but in his nervousness he made a mess of it: in the event of a puddle, head for a crash.

Somewhere behind Jack, somebody wondered aloud if there was an Air Marshal on the flight. Jack turned to the person next to him, a smiling old woman who was beginning to wish her children had not moved so far away.

"It ain't me, babe," he said, trying to sound relaxed.

She smiled. "I saw Bob Dylan when he was starting out, in Greenwich Village. You know, he couldn't even tune his own guitar. Liam Clancy had to do it for him. He had such a baby face in those days. You probably don't even know who Liam Clancy is."

Jack could see the next eight hours turning into a lecture on how she came to be alone. He was glad he could truthfully answer yes, he knew who Liam Clancy was. As a child, Jack had listened to Makem and Clancy records.

"Irish folk singer."

"Good for you," the old woman said. "Well, did you know, Tommy Makem's mother was also a singer, and the songs she taught her son had a big influence on Bob Dylan. Isn't that amazing?"

"What?"

"Isn't it amazing that an old woman singing songs in her kitchen in Ireland could influence the folk revival in the nineteen sixties? And that influenced everything that came after it. Jimi Hendrix was nearly beaten up because he liked Bob Dylan, and don't forget David Bowie."

"Yeah?"

"Have you ever heard *The Buddha of Suburbia*?"

"No."

"Oh now, it's pure mighty."

For a couple of hours, she regaled him with stories, not a trace of sadness in her voice. She had not kept up with anything after The Clash, although she liked Nick Cave, and KT Tunstall could sing the phone book, and, she leaned in towards Jack and whispered, "Isn't she a little ride?" She winked.

After they had eaten, Jack settled back and finally fell asleep. He slept until he felt a soft hand on his shoulder. A gentle English voice called him back to consciousness.

"Sir, sir?"

Jack opened his eyes and looked up into the flight attendant's orange face, a million miles away from the voice that always sounded so cultured.

"Are we there?" he asked.

"No sir, we're coming into Shannon."

"OK. Thank you."

He sat up straight and for a moment watched her walk away, watched her blue skirt sculpting her backside into perfection. He turned his attention to the view outside. Ireland. He had never been, but like most of Irish-America, he had been raised on stories of the Glorious Revolution. Every few years they would hear of a bomb going off in Belfast. They knew the IRA would never do something like that on purpose, so most of Irish-America assumed the bomb had gone off by accident. This assumption allowed them to continue to support and help to fund murderers. As a child, Jack imagined Northern Ireland as a vast garden: A place where craggy-faced old men planted bombs in rows, and every day, lovingly tended to their crop in anticipation of spring. When he grew old enough to reason, Jack found these stories ludicrous. He once asked his grandfather, an old IRA man, why someone would plant a bomb if he did not want to kill anyone. He received a smack in the face for his curiosity.

As the plane touched down, Jack could see American soldiers and warplanes.

"Isn't that a terrible sight?" the old woman said.

Jack jumped at the sound of her voice. He had forgotten about her. He gave no answer. He saw no need for the question. He turned back to the window. He could just about see a small camp outside the fence, populated by protesters. The Irish Government had decided that neutrality, as enshrined in the constitution, was aspirational, and this allowed the militarization of Shannon Airport.

Jack laughed, when Ireland was governed by a schoolteacher, neutrality was sacrosanct, but in the Ireland of an accountant, neutrality is aspirational.

The old woman shook her head, "Why is Bertie Ahern still at large? He's an awful gobshite. But he's as lucky as a cut cat."

The passengers began to disembark. "Well," the old

woman said, "I'm off now to Stab City to see my daughter. It was lovely talking to you. Enjoy the rest of your trip."

"And you," said Jack. Over his shoulder, he could hear the ghost of his grandfather dismissing the protestors as *Shitehawks*. Jack sympathized with the protestors, but he wondered how many had been there throughout the Cold War, when Shannon Airport was used by both the American and Soviet military. The instant Jack had that thought, he realized Ireland's neutrality was a con. It had never existed. The Schoolteacher had signed the book of condolence for Adolph Hitler.

As he waited for his flight to London, Jack saw a gulfstream jet takeoff. Was it one of the torture planes? He recalled the words of Condoleezza Rice, "Where appropriate, the United States seeks assurances that transported persons will not be tortured." Jack translated this as, "It would be inappropriate for the United States to seek assurances that transported persons will not be tortured, when those persons are being transported in order to be tortured."

Jack sometimes wondered if he had been right to vote for Dubya.

Peter Hopkins – II

September brought school, and for Peter's crowd: a shift from the manly pursuits of boys to the manly pursuit of girls. Over the summer, one of the friends had seen his first porn movie. With horrified fascination, he watched a fifty-year-old man have sex with a twelve-year-old girl. Now, the friend recounted this movie as if he had lived it. He told how he had overcome her resistance, "You gotta slap 'em around a bit, they expect it." He laughed as he described her screams while he forced his "twelve inches of rock solid man-meat into her warm wet cunt *oh yeah!*" He sniffed his fingers, "Hmm, fish sticks."

Listening to the intimate details of this rape, Peter was as horrified as his friend had been watching the movie.

They were joined by another friend who looked at them with knowing contempt. He accused, "You're a homo, you're a homo, you're a homo."

One of the three flared up. "You better not be calling me a faggot."

This brought laughter from the third but left Peter confused. The only faggots he knew about were bundles of twigs tied together and used as kindling.

"Homosapien. Latin for man. Faggots are people who write poetry."

Peter felt suddenly isolated. He knew now that he was *a being apart*, that though he occupied the same world as his school friends, he was something more. Poetry had made him dangerous. He made a mental note to check on what, precisely, was meant by *Faggot*.

At home that evening, he found a message from *The UniVerse*. He stood looking at the envelope, almost afraid to touch it. The sound of his mother's footsteps hurried him on.

Peter made a beeline for his room. He locked himself in and sat on the bed nervously waiting for the perfect moment to find out what had been decided. He opened the envelope and delicately withdrew the white paper. He read, trying not to shout. His work would appear in the next issue of the magazine.

In a bid to encourage young writers, the editors had decided to add a section for poets who, though not yet fully formed, held out a promise for the future. A poem would be published, and more experienced writers invited to review it. Peter put the letter aside, picked it up again and reread it, hardly believing a word. He picked up the poem that had been accepted. He went through it line by line searching for anything that might be wrong.

Anthony Chapman

Song of the Pilgrim Soul

Say goodbye to all you hold
Sacred – goodbye to all you think
You know – your father's time
Has been and gone and so
Be gone.

Say goodbye to all your schemes
And treasons, goodbye to all
Your plans, your mother's eyes
Will dry in the dust
Kicked from your heels.

Leave the others to their decorations –

>   calendar
>   holy books
>   lavender
>   stop.

Leave your women to their simple logic –
>   your men to their sacred cows

Let your children reach their understanding –
Live only the life that is in you now –

Find yourself bewildered beyond reason
Drinking deep of all you can't explain

Through this breach true faith now slowly slips
To wrest the law from your human heart.

06/The Company of Thieves

From his first footfall on British soil, Jack's every move was monitored. The same man in grey who had walked in his footsteps at the Whitely Museum cleared Jack's way through customs. The same Anonymous Angel had someone sitting in the foyer of the Dorchester Hotel, glancing over the Financial Times as Jack checked in, and a bellboy carried his bags to the lift.

Jack stepped into his Mayfair Suite. It seemed a little girly. Floral patterns dominated throughout the three rooms: sitting room, bedroom, and bathroom. French windows opened onto a balcony with views of Mayfair and Park Lane.

This was a London unknown to Jack and so, uncertain of the etiquette, he gave the bellboy a big tip. Then, just in case British prejudice expected it, Jack decided to be crass.

"Is this the same room that Eisenhower stayed in?"

The bellboy thought for a moment before replying with a confident, "Yes Sir, of course."

After a long hot shower, Jack climbed in between the Irish linen sheets and let the wilderness on the bedclothes engulf him. He slept soundly and awoke in darkness, with a cold breeze blowing through the suite. He got out of bed and went through to the sitting room to find the French windows open. He closed them, showered and dressed. He unpacked his bags and poured a glass of Tullamore Dew; he almost didn't drink it; then he threw it back and called room service.

"I don't think so, sir." Jack had just informed them that he was Mr. Higgins in the Eisenhower Suite.

"Look, I just need some food."

"Yes sir, what would you like?"

"Can you send up some scrambled eggs, bacon, toast, and coffee?"

"I don't think so, sir."

"Excuse me?"

"Sir, breakfast was eight hours ago. If you'd care to wait until morning, I'm sure we can accommodate you."

"No, I wouldn't care to wait until morning."

"Perhaps sir would care for an omelette?"

"No, sir would not care for an omelette. You have the eggs, right?"

"Yes sir, we have the eggs."

"Then here's what you do. Take a couple of eggs, put them in a pan, whisk them, cook them, and send them up. OK!"

Jack sat at a small table in the crowded dining area of a pavement café. The people at the other tables appeared to be bankers and young fashionistas, jaded by the world, or excited over nothing. Snatches of conversation floated by. There was no way to tell who was discussing what, but the so-called war on terror and reality TV went hand in hand, both of them dressed in this season's black.

A waiter arrived at Jack's table. On the waiter's raised hand was a tray, and on that tray, a plate held a hero sandwich. He lifted the plate off the tray and put it down on the table. Jack's eyes followed. He looked up at the waiter.

"That's not what I ordered."

A woman's voice spoke. "I ordered it."

Jack turned to the voice, and his body instantly convulsed, as if he had just been punched in the heart. He fell forward onto the table, almost tipping it over. The woman dropped down to examine him. She called to the crowd, "Any of you people a Doctor?"

The other diners had turned; some shocked, some frightened, some irritated by the noise, some became concerned for the stranger's welfare, but nobody wanted to get involved.

The woman turned to the waiter, "Get some water." He went back inside, and a moment later two others came out to look. The woman continued her examination of Jack. His pulse had returned to normal by the time the water arrived. He accepted it thankfully and sipped between deep breaths. He sat back. Looking at her now, Jack found himself captured by a woman who excited everything in him.

"What happened?" Her face still insisted on his wellbeing. Jack did not answer. He was afraid to speak in case the terror in his bones told in his voice.

"Are you OK?" she asked.

"Yes," said Jack. "Yes. I'm sorry. It was. Just." He waved whatever it was away. His body filled with those sensations that make all other excitements irrelevant. This excitement surpassed the need for a beautiful face and figure. Although hers were damn good, she had something more. She aroused feelings in Jack that he had avoided for years. There was terror at the heart of what he felt. He pushed his chair back a little in order to take her in more fully.

She appeared to be in her early thirties, old-money-American. When she spoke, there was the barest hint of England in her accent. She introduced herself as Sarah. She stood for a moment, waiting, and then sat down and started to reassemble the sandwich. Jack was still shaking inside, afraid and uncertain about how to continue with the job. Sarah took a bite of the sandwich and held it out to Jack.

"Hm? No. Thank you. I'm waiting on something."

"You're sure you're OK?"

"Yeah, yeah, I'm fine, it's just, delayed reaction, I

guess."

"Delayed reaction to what?"

"Nothing."

"OK." She could see him struggling to make eye contact. She had known many men in Jack's profession, but none had been afraid of her.

"How are you enjoying London?" she asked.

"I just arrived."

"Well, make sure you get to the Tate. They've got a broken light."

"A broken light?"

"Yeah, it's art, apparently. An empty room with a light that flickers on and off, I don't know what it's supposed to mean. But ..." She shrugged.

"I'll pass. I've seen broken lights before. They're not that interesting."

"You don't like modern art?"

"I don't get it," he said, thankful for the diversion. "You ever see that shark in a tank? 'The Physical Impossibility of Death in the Mind of Someone Living.' What's that? It's a dead shark."

"Well, I suppose you have to do these things."

"No. You don't."

"You're just a hired goon, huh? Just here for the money?"

"What are you here for?"

"That's my business."

Jack's food arrived: fried cheese and chips. They ate in silence. Jack used his dinner as an excuse not to look at Sarah. She finished her sandwich and took a mouthful of coffee. She took a TV guide out of her shoulder bag and leafed through it.

"Have you ever seen the Jeremy Kyle show?" she asked.

"I've never heard of it."

"A judge said it's like a human form of bear-baiting. I guess he's right. It's like Springer. You've seen Springer?"

"I've heard of him."

"But never seen him?"

"No."

"My God, you really don't have any time for culture," she joked. "It's Rednecks bitching and beating each other up while Jerry prods them in the right direction and tries not to laugh. Then at the end of the show, Jerry gives his final thought. A little moral tag."

"A moral tag?"

"It's what pornographers used to do in the old days."

"Porn with a moral?" He laughed.

"Yeah," Sarah said, "that way, when the censors question the artistic merits of a blue-eyed blonde cheerleader having sex with the winner of the Kentucky Derby, and I mean the horse, the filmmakers can point to their little morality tag. 'The sex organs of a blue-eyed blonde cheerleader were never intended to accommodate the sex organs of Seabiscuit. The young woman you've just been watching, never walked again.' It's kind of like ancient Rome. Springer, Kyle, all those people. It's basically a sort of pornography. He's on in an hour."

Jack went to the toilet, when he returned Sarah was reaching out to hail a cab. Her outstretched arm pulled the grey woollen dress tighter to the contours of her body. Again, Jack felt a thrill of terror. He saw her naked. He saw himself waking up beside her. He began to name the children. But he knew this was not a woman with whom he should get involved. He walked up to her just as a cab pulled in. Sarah turned, "Nice meeting you," she said. They shook hands.

"I thought we were going to watch Jeremy Kyle."

"Oh, that was just empty talk," Sarah said. She got into the cab and was gone.

Jack opened the French windows of his hotel suite. He filled a tumbler with Tullamore Dew. He picked up the drink and noticed ripples break against the side of the glass. He realised his hand was shaking. He stared at it, using all of his concentration to will it steady. When he had regained control, Jack put the glass down.

He went into the bathroom and washed his hands. He splashed water on his face and stood before the mirror wondering what, if anything, had happened.

Coming out of the bathroom, he put a hand into one of his pockets and felt something: a piece of folded paper. He took it out, unfolded it and read, "I have your wallet. The hotel bar, ten PM. Wear a suit." Sudden panic held him. He wanted to run, but he didn't know where. He went to the table, picked up the glass of whisky and downed it in one.

Jack laughed. Sarah. He could think of no opportunity she'd had to pick his pocket. He opened a bottle of mineral water and drank it down to dilute the whisky. He stepped out onto the balcony. The sound of Nat King Cole drifted by, carried along Park Lane by his perfect phrasing. It felt like a counterpoint to this murkier world into which Jack had been thrust.

Jack carried the song with him to the hotel bar. He stood at the door, surveying the crowd. He felt like a spy about to enter enemy territory. The bar was full of older men with younger women, younger men with older women, and couples who looked as if they had been together forever. A few of these looked as if they still liked each other. The room represented Jack's livelihood, people, he long ago decided, who never had to stand in line to pay a few bucks off a bill; people who trotted out worthless statements like, "I put my trousers on one leg at a time, just like everybody else." in an attempt to show ... what?

Jack pushed the thought aside; his prejudice would not get the job done. He stepped fully into the room and began making his way to the bar.

Sarah wore a golden dress that fell off her shoulders and made her face, in profile, resemble the portraits of aristocratic young women one sometimes sees framed in gaudy ovals. She threw her head back, laughing as the man beside her leaned in and whispered something. His finger touched her shoulder in an attempt at seduction.

On impulse, she pulled away. "Easy tiger."

"Good evening," said Jack.

The man beside Sarah turned to Jack. "Can I help you with something?"

"Jack." Sarah smiled. "I'm sorry," she said to the tiger, "it would never work. I'd only break your heart."

"That's not what I'm after sweetheart."

She turned to Jack, "Shall we?" It was ten o'clock. As they left the bar, she said, "It's a pity; he was only killing time until the Tokyo gets up. What time is it in Tokyo?"

"I have no idea."

A black limousine sat waiting outside the hotel. The driver, standing by the back door, dropped his cigarette when he saw Jack and Sarah approach. He nodded to Sarah and opened the door. She and Jack climbed into the car, and the door softly closed. There were five others in the limo. Darkness had reshaped their faces, making them impossible to read. They appeared to be ordinary executives. Jack felt jealous of the time they had spent with Sarah. He laughed at his own stupidity. This was business; he was her job, but, possibly because of his reaction when they met, he hoped for some kind of fidelity. Ludicrous, he knew, but he still hoped. Sarah sat at the driver's end and pressed a button, closing the window that divided the two parts of the car.

"Gentlemen," she said as the car pulled away, "for the benefit of the newcomer, there is to be no talking. You are not to share any personal information with each other. You are not to share any professional information with each other. We are now going to view the item, after which you will report to your employers. If it becomes necessary, in the interest of security, our driver is armed. Do I make myself clear?" Sarah looked at the grim shadows. She stopped when she came to Jack. He was staring at her, wondering where this new woman had come from. He raised his hand.

"Yes?" Sarah asked.

"What if I have to use the restroom?" Jack was joking, but the others nodded agreement.

"Cross your legs," Sarah replied.

Jack smiled. He imagined his way past the job, to the woman he wanted her to be, and then told himself to stop being stupid.

Sarah continued, "The personal effects that were taken from you will be returned when you get back to your hotel rooms. Now," her voice softened a little. "I have a gift for each of you." She unlocked a drawer beside her and took out six black velvet bags. She passed them to her charges. "Put them on and pull the string."

They did as instructed, they were under orders; otherwise they would never have accepted this humiliation. The journey continued in silence. Beneath his hood, Jack listened for any clue as to where they were going. Gradually the sound of the city slipped away, leaving only the hum of the engine, and the greater hum of his cheap aftershave, which now had an accent of sweat. His hair itched. His right leg went to sleep and he could feel the beginnings of a cramp in the small of his back. He shifted in his seat and began to flex his leg, attempting to exercise it back to life.

Some hours later, the limo slowed down and turned off the main road. They were now driving on an old track. An occasional pothole bumped the passengers around in their seats. A telephone buzzed into life. Jack could hear the vibrations carry it along the counter before the soft slap of Sarah's hand muffled the sound. There was a slight click. Then Sarah's voice, "Yes." After a pause, there came the louder click of the phone being closed. A few minutes later the limo stopped. Jack heard a door open and close as someone got out. Moments later the door beside Jack opened, he felt a big hand grasp his forearm and help him out of the car. He began to take the bag off his head, but a big voice, presumably belonging to the big hands said, "No."

Waiting while the others were helped out of the car, Jack heard Sarah's voice say, "Not you." The air filled with an explosive stillness, as if they had just entered a war zone.

"Whadda ya mean, not me?"

There was the sound of a scuffle, then silence, then footsteps, then a dull thump, and then there were five. The men now standing in line were instructed to hold hands. Inside the hoods, their heads turned on impulse, looking for confirmation that there was nothing queer about holding hands. As each man realised he was alone, nervous fingers reached out and pulled back as they touched other nervous fingers. Then hand slipped into hand, bringing, to some of the men, fear of what was a sensual intimacy. Others squeezed hands in a little power play, taking a measure of comfort from the sweaty palms that collapsed in theirs.

They were led away from the car and up five steps. A hand reached out and bent each man's head as he entered through a low doorway. The words "Not you" still playing in their ears, caused some of them to wonder would they make it through the night. When each man was seated again, the door was closed, and Sarah's voice came over the PA system, "You can take the hoods off now."

They were in the cabin of a Gulfstream jet. All but one of the lights had been removed. The five men looked at each other, trying to size one another up. Jack turned to the window, he tried to open the shade but it was sealed. The others were the same. They never knew how long they were in the air, but at some point the sound of Sarah's voice instructed them to put the bags back over their heads.

The next time they removed the bags, they were in a

large concrete room, the walls painted to resemble marble, the floor painted to resemble mahogany. Chairs arranged around the room looked beautiful and uncomfortable. They were copies of a chair designed as an artwork in nineteen fifteen and now worth millions. These chairs, although identical in every way except age, were just uncomfortable.

Mona Lisa, radiant in the company of thieves, looked down on the gathering from a small stage. Jack sat down; he had no interest in the painting. He was there simply to show his face until he had to bid.

There were twenty people in the room. Some sat waiting for whatever was going to happen. Others, attempting to look like what television called 'street punks' explored the painting.

"No, no, no."

"I'm telling you, she's got someone chowing down on her."

"Chowing down on her?"

"Yeah."

"Eating that?"

"I read it in a magazine."

"You read it in a magazine?"

"Yeah."

"Well, you know what they say about them muff divers."

A harsh laugh broke from the other man. "Why not?"

"Why not? Let me tell you who eats pussy. Pussies and Fags is all the people who eats pussy. Pussies and Fags."

"Pussies and Fags?"

"Pussies and Fags. So if you're telling me that you eat pussy, then you tell me which one are you. A Pussy or a Fag."

A violent silence. A murderous smile. A practiced laugh. They were the representatives of the most powerful men in the world. They shook hands.

At the back of the room, heavy oak doors opened.

"Gentlemen," Sarah said. "If you would take your seats."

As they sat down, Sarah led a procession to the stage. Behind her followed an old man in an exquisitely tailored suit that fit him better than his own skin. He held onto the arm of a second man. Two younger men followed: each of them built like a Nazi experiment. Something in the old man's appearance suggested to Jack that he was blind. This seemed to be confirmed when they reached the stage. The old man's companion whispered into his ear. He stepped up onto the stage and was led across to the only comfortable chair in the room.

"Gentlemen." Sarah began. "I would like to introduce Mr. de Valfierno. It was Mr de Valfierno's father, Eduardo de Valfierno who masterminded the acquisition of this piece." A round of applause sounded like rain on a tin roof. Shining eyes focused on the legend in the chair. The old man turned to the sound and nodded his acceptance of the tribute. Jack joined in with the applause, but felt only contempt: an old gangster is merely someone who aspired to evil with greater success that those who died young. Jack pictured a Europe filled with anonymous graves, each occupied by silenced assassins, advisors, critics, and the innocent who had simply been in the wrong place at the wrong time. He made a mental note to check the genealogy of Eduardo de Valfierno.

In nineteen fifty, a honeymoon couple disappeared. They had been walking through Montmartre. The man pointed out a bar where, during the war, he had gotten drunk with Picasso, who paid for drinks with stories of his heroic youth. These stories now brought gales of joyous laughter from the soldier's bride. That night, on the orders of a young gangster who had been sitting at a table outside the bar, and who had decided their laughter was directed at him, the honeymooner's bones were cleaned of all flesh, washed, dried and stacked in the catacombs.

Twenty years later, the son this GI left in Italy photographed another young honeymoon couple. What no one knew is that the bride was the photographer's half sister from Arkansas, born to the woman who had given her virginity as a parting gift to a young soldier, living up his final furlough, on his way to World War 2.

The GI never knew of his children, the children never knew of their father.

Now a grandmother, she still sometimes sits with the photograph, recalling the girl that she was, standing so proud and happy beside her man. On those occasions that she notices the skull resting just above her right shoulder, it never occurs to her that the father she never knew was watching over her young love.

As he looked at the old man, Jack found a sickening irony in the bloodless hands so drenched in blood, in the sightless eyes that had for so long seen them coming.

"Before we proceed," Sarah said. "I would like you to take note," she paused, making sure she had everybody's attention, "these are the men with the guns." She indicated the two men standing either side of the painting. There was a noise at the back of the room. The audience turned and watched a security guard wheel a trolley draped in black velvet up to the stage. One of the men who flanked the painting removed it from the easel and put it down out of sight. He picked a rectangular object, still covered with the velvet, from the trolley, set it on the easel and stood back.

"Gentlemen," Sarah said. She pulled back the velvet, "The Mona Lisa."

During World War 2, the Mona Lisa had been hidden away for safety. What happened to it during that time?

An X-ray examination would show three versions of the painting beneath the final one. She had once worn a bonnet and clutched the arms of the chair in which she sat.

Her right elbow had been partially restored. At her left elbow, there should be the ghost of a mark left by a stone thrown at her in nineteen fifty-six, as though she were some kind of harlot, but her hair did not hang loosely, it was fixed in place, marking her out as a woman of substance. There were the peculiarities of the timber to consider. How far had the paint penetrated the poplar in five hundred years? The painting had an eleven-millimetre groove in it. Yet even if the front of the painting were exactly as it should be, would the back withstand the same scrutiny? If this painting had all of those signatures, then which one was real and which fake; the aristocrat hanging in Paris; the one they were faced with now? Then there was her smile. That famous, enigmatic, Mona Lisa smile.

Her smile had been analyzed using emotion recognition software. It broke down as eighty-three percent happy, nine percent disgusted, six percent fearful, two percent angry and less than one percent neutral and not surprised at all. An American academic had stated that her smile could only be viewed peripherally. It disappeared if you looked directly at it. This had something to do with the way the eye works. But of the multitudes that daily came to worship, gawking at the back of somebody's head, how many would wait to stand alone, before the bullet proof glass and look, both peripherally and directly at her, to see if her smile really did disappear? Or would they just tick this young Florentine woman off their list of cultural experiences? Part of Jack's brain told him that these concerns were needless nit-picking, but he would feel better if the painting was a forgery. The idea of Masterson pawing the body of this expectant mother made Jack's flesh crawl. He could picture the lascivious hands caress her pregnancy, the twisted look in the old man's eyes, burning from the unnaturally smooth face, the counterfeit of youth waging war on the real thing.

"Before we begin the authentication," Sarah continued,

"Mr. de Valfierno thought you might appreciate some background information on just how much this painting is worth."

There was movement on the floor as the bidders sat to attention. This was what they had travelled half way round the world for.

"During nineteen sixty-two and nineteen sixty-three, the painting was on loan to the United States. Prior to that tour, the painting was assessed for insurance purposes."

Sarah stopped talking; she checked to see she had the full attention of the room. When she felt all eyes upon her, she said, "The painting was valued at one hundred million dollars. This makes it the most valuable painting ever insured."

Sarah looked out over her audience, smiling as she watched the effect of her words. The paraphernalia of extreme wealth danced in the minds of some of those present. Bodies shifted in chairs; muscles tensed and relaxed, here and there, a forehead became beaded with sweat, and eyes became sharply focused.

"As some of you may be aware," she paused, letting the excitement build, "there are three other paintings which have surpassed this amount. Adele Bloch-Bauer I by Gustav Klimt sold for one hundred and thirty-five million dollars. This time last year, Woman III, by Willem de Kooning sold for one hundred and thirty-seven point five million dollars, and painting No. 5 1948, by Jackson Pollock sold for the record price of one hundred and forty million dollars.

"However, those were all recent sales. When you adjust the nineteen sixty-two figures, this Lady here, is worth almost seven hundred million dollars."

Sarah enjoyed the delight that spread from face to face; the hands that gripped the arms of chairs: Strip Club hands, afraid to risk the kind of punishment they had sanctioned for others. Seven hundred million dollars to hang upon the wall.

"And now," Sarah said.

De Valfierno's assistant removed the painting to a bank of machines. Sarah touched the screen of her palm pilot and the wall behind her opened up, revealing a seventy-one inch monitor. She touched her palm pilot a second time, and the room darkened. Onto the screen came an image of the Mona Lisa from which the colour slowly drained. As the image changed, Sarah conducted the eyes of the crowd, drawing them to individual signatures, explaining the absence of others: proof that the painting was real.

Some of those watching grew bored, restless and hungry for popcorn and beer. Others became thoughtful, carefully considering what they were seeing. As interesting as they found it, it was, after all, only a movie. Watching the faces that he could see, Jack had to remind himself that just because someone is an amoral sociopath, it does not automatically make him a half-wit. The painting may have been worth seven hundred million dollars, but it was still just a painting, a painting of which ownership could never be acknowledged. In the eyes of some, that made it worthless, but they were there to do a job. Someone's boss would be happy to hide her away, and on those days when running his empire was murder, he could come home at night and relax with a private show. He may already have a room prepared, with the exact conditions – light, humidity – all set to prevent any further degradation of his secret pleasure, this woman for whom he had paid so much money.

Hours of evidence later, Sarah stopped. She let the room's attention fall on her once more. "Gentlemen," she said, "you have your authentication."

She felt tired and energized in equal measure. Obscure ideas flowered and died and bloomed again in a different colour. She experienced the strange sensation of having two brains in her head, one behind the other. With the front brain, she had made the presentation. With the other, hidden brain, she had guided her performance, pouring more and more energy into the crowd until they could not but be in love with her. She had opened herself up to the ugly embrace of the room without letting it touch her.

The old man in his leather armchair began to applaud. He was suddenly full of authority. He had acquired a presence that belied his slight frame. He turned to the room, imposing himself on them until their applause drown out his own.

"Gentlemen," Sarah repeated, "you have your authentication. The sale will take place one week from tonight. Are there any questions?"

The man who had earlier explained his theory of cunnilingus stood up.

"Yeah. How do we know you didn't just fake that?"

The room went silent. Expectant faces turned to the stage.

"As I've said, you have your authentication. If any of you would like to drop out now, please feel free to do so."

07/Loneliness

Jack closed the door of his hotel suite. He was tired beyond the possibility of sleep. He sat on the arm of the couch, took off his shoes and socks, flexed his toes and massaged his feet. He went over to the window and peeked through the curtains for anyone who might be watching the room. Suddenly he felt ridiculous. He drew back the curtains and watched the sun turn the sky a delicate blue. For a moment, he was back in his apartment, standing before the savannah in the hallway. He thought he saw Sarah down in the street. Her voice was music, and now Jack knew he was in trouble. He felt the impossibility of anything happening between them; he wondered if there was a way that something might.

He felt the need to get laid, and then recalled Masterson's words, "Why does a man like you support the slave trade?"

Now, for the first time, Jack saw the ugly reality of his sex life: the buying and selling of flesh. His eyes closed, and his head turned away from a memory moving within him: a sweet face and the sweeter tones of Tennessee.

When loneliness got the better of him, Jack searched through the listings of Elegant Company, looking for a woman who was free for the evening. The website informed prospective clients that they were paying for companionship and conversation. Anything else that happened was a coincidence and a private matter between consenting adults. Beneath the disclaimer, there was a list of what might happen as a coincidence between consenting adults. For a few hundred dollars, he could empty himself into some anonymous body. For a few thousand dollars, she would spend the night, and Jack would not have to wake up alone. He recalled a conversation. "We need to set some ground rules," she said. "You can make love with me in my butt and in my mouth, but until there's a ring on this finger, only Jesus gets to Yee-Haw my McGraw. We clear?"

The following morning, he woke to find her sitting up in bed, her knees and the covers pulled up to her chin. She looked at him with the eyes of a penitent and spoke with the voice of a child, "I need you to pee on my face."

Jack was shocked, not by her request, but by his ability to comply.

Right now, whores would be too much of a complication. He went to the table and poured a drink. He pulled a chair over to the windows and relaxed into the cushions, the whisky, and the fresh breeze. He cursed himself for trusting that Clarence had packed a few books.

He began to doze off. The glass slipped from his hand, and the whisky spilled onto his lap. His eyes opened when the glass hit the floor, and he sat up wondering where he was. He looked down at the familiar stain spreading out from his crotch. He pulled his trousers away from his skin and only then recognised the smell. He laughed, happy that for once, he was wrong. He stood up and took his trousers off. He threw them over the back of the chair. There was something he had planned to do. Yes. He went to the bedroom and wrote a note: Check out the genealogy of Eduardo De Valfierno.

Jack's hands began to shake. His heart began to race. He could feel a cold sweat on his face. Part of this was the lack of sleep, part the lack of preparation. On his other jobs, he had time to prepare; he could minimise the variables. On this job, he did not even know what the variables were, and now, he discovered he was hungry.

He called room service and ordered breakfast, telling them to leave it in the room if he did not answer. Then Jack remembered his wallet. Sarah had stolen his wallet. He glanced around the sitting room, expecting the wallet to be within view; he checked the bedroom and the bathroom. He tried to imagine someone coming into the room with the wallet and putting it – it was no use, he was too tired. He could cancel his credit cards with a phone call. He had ready cash in safety deposit boxes throughout Europe. That left the wallet itself; a prize Jack had allowed himself on his first job.

He took a shower to pass the time, leaning against the wall while the needles of hot water attacked him. In the back of his mind, Jack could hear a drumming sound that he was unable to place. Then he heard another noise. Was it in the room or on the street?

Jack stepped out of the shower. He shivered and listened at the bathroom door. He began to turn the handle. He closed his eyes to feel his way and then slowly pulled open the door. The living-room curtains were drawn, and the jungle looked restful in soft light. Someone coughed in the bedroom. Sarah? Jack put on a robe and tiptoed to the bedroom door. Another cough. He looked for a weapon and noticed his stained trousers draped over the chair. He saw the whisky bottle on the table. Another cough. Footsteps to the bedroom door. Jack gripped the handle. The heavy steps presented an Ogre to Jack's mind. He threw his entire weight against the door and slammed it closed.

A roar of pain. Stumbling footsteps tripped, and a body hit the floor. Jack swung the door open. He stepped into the bedroom. A man had begun to stand up. Jack knocked him down, rolled him onto his stomach and sat on his back. He screamed.

"What the fuck –"

Jack pulled his arms up behind his back, almost to the breaking point.

"You have twenty seconds to tell me what you're doing here."

A terrified voice spoke. "I brought your suit back."

"What?"

"I brought your suit back."

Jack looked around the bedroom. "I don't see any suit."

"I hung it up. It's in the wardrobe."

Jack looked again at the man beneath him. A hotel uniform, but that meant nothing: uniforms are easy to come by.

"Why is the other room dark? Why didn't you turn on the lights?"

"I didn't need the lights. The windows were open."

"Why did you close them?"

"It was raining."

"What?"

"It's pissing down out there."

The drumming in the back of Jack's mind now softened into the sound of rain. He leaned back, let go of the other man's arms and turned to the window. He watched the curling vines on the curtains, half-expecting water to drip from the leaves, a Rainforest in London. From somewhere he heard a voice, "Can I get up now?" Jack looked at the body beneath him. He could not have been more than twenty-three, a kid. What was he doing in this mess? He should be more scared. He began to move.

Jack pushed the kid's head into the carpet and patted his hand along the body. The kid didn't even have a mobile phone.

"OK," said Jack, "I'm going to let you go in a moment. I'm trusting you. If you try anything." He gave the kid's arms a little push to remind him of the pain he would be in. "Are we clear?"

"Yes, yes, we're clear. We're clear."

Jack placed the kid's arms by his side and held them there a moment. He stood up and stepped back.

"OK, get up."

The kid struggled to his feet. He stepped away from Jack and stood nursing his shoulders. He picked a point on the floor and stared at it, waiting for the danger to pass.

"Look at me," Jack ordered, and the kid snapped to attention. "When did I give you that suit?"

"I don't know. I was just told to bring it back."

"Get it."

"What?"

"Get the suit."

As the kid obeyed, Jack said, "I didn't send a suit out to be cleaned."

The kid handed the suit to Jack. He looked it over. It was his suit.

"Over there." Jack pointed to the far side of the room. The kid waited.

"Now," Jack said.

The kid edged his way across the room. Jack went to the telephone. As he disconnected it, he said, "I'm gonna check on something, and if everything's OK, everything's OK. You can sit down if you like."

The kid sat on the floor. Jack shook his head. He took the telephone lead and the suit and went to the sitting room. He closed and locked the bedroom door.

Jack searched the suit pockets and found his wallet. Everything was intact. He dressed and went to unlock the bedroom door. As he turned the key, he heard the kid moving about and decided he was getting ready to attack. Jack pushed the door open and stood away.

In the bedroom, the kid had picked up the telephone, intending to use it as a weapon. When he heard the key turn in the lock, he scrambled away. The door opened, and the kid panicked. He dropped the telephone. He waited for the crazy Yank to come in. When he didn't, the kid began to feel threatened by the open door. After a few minutes, he told himself, "Maybe the fucking arsehole's gone back to America." He took a step and waited, listening. Another step. Two steps. Three. He listened. He stepped into the doorway. Shit! The crazy Yank was waiting for him.

"How are you feeling?" Jack asked.

The kid's eyes replied, "Fuck off."

"Are you a boxer?"

"No."

"Well then, you'll be OK." Jack took two hundred pounds from his wallet and gave it to the kid.

"That's your tip," he said.

Then, taking another two hundred from the wallet, added, "Here's another one."

The kid reached for the money; Jack snapped it away. "No-one is to hear about what happened here. Understand?"

"Yes."

"Yes, what?"

"Yes, Sir?"

"No."

"Oh. Oh, no one is to hear about what happened here."

"Good." Jack handed over the money.

"Can I go now?"

That night, at one of London's open-mic sessions, a young comedian enjoyed his first success, telling the tale of the naked Yank who mugged him for a tuxedo.

08/Brief Encounter

Tearing down the road, Jack hardly felt the acceleration. There were two lanes; traffic came on one side and went on the other. Tonight, his was the only car. He pushed his foot down and thrilled to the needle passing seventy, eighty, ninety, one hundred miles per hour. *This was driving.* His new car had been delivered that day, and he had taken her out for a spin.

The sound of Bon Jovi filled the car, spilled out through the open windows and proclaimed to the world that we were *'Livin' on a Prayer.'*

Red lights on the highway. This was what he wanted. Jack found beauty in the line of cars ahead. He moved into the oncoming lane. Swollen with the excitement of his increasing speed, his hand flat on the horn, Jack tore past the first few cars.

Light spread like rapid dawn through the trees and sky. The sound of Jack's car horn was drowned out by the greater sound of an oncoming truck. Yes! He speeded up, racing straight towards the truck. Then, as the world turned white, Jack pulled back into his own lane and turned the music up. The other cars soon disappeared from view, half a state behind him. Jack continued racing through Bon Jovi and Def Leppard. By the time he met Sarah, he was singing along to Black Sabbath's *Country Girl.* Then he met her, briefly, before she took flight and his car careered out of control, slamming into a small sedan broken down by the side of the road. The last thing Jack saw before losing consciousness was an angel hit the ground.

Jack awoke, frightened and crying for the woman he had killed, and for her pregnancy. He tried to keep still, hoping the thing in the dark would leave him alone. He was unsure that what had happened in his dream had happened in his life. It took a minute for his tears to be stopped by the certainty that, yes, it had happened. He had killed a woman and her unborn child.

Jack got out of bed. His routine after this dream was to exercise. He did fifty slow push-ups, physical strain to distract his body, to help distract his mind. He focused completely on performing each movement, breathing out as he pushed up, breathing in as he lowered himself to the floor. He was waiting for a burst of endorphins. When it came, when he escaped his past, he got up, safe until he dreamed again.

On the bedside locker, Jack found a note: Check out the genealogy of Eduardo de Valfierno.

In a small internet café, Jack Googled Eduardo De Valfierno. He was, allegedly, an Argentine con man who referred to himself as 'Marquis'. His career appeared to consist entirely of the Mona Lisa fraud. Jack found a link to an old Shirley MacLaine and Michael Caine movie called *Gambit*, which told basically the same story as de Valfierno's adventure. Digging a little deeper, Jack discovered that there is no evidence de Valfierno ever existed. The stories about him only go back to the nineteen thirties. Jack stopped, his finger hovering above the mouse: the sale was a fake. From Jack's perspective, this changed nothing, without further instructions he would just have to carry on, and for now he would have to keep his mouth shut. His finger fell, and the screen came alive with the descendants of Lisa Gherardini, one of them almost a dead ringer for her famous ancestor. Behind Jack, a familiar voice spoke, "Oh that's good."

Sarah pulled a chair over to Jack. Instinctively he moved away. His elbow hit the mouse and the picture on the screen changed. It now showed a woman dancing at a formal ball, the flourish of her blue dress was like a burst of electricity in the hide-bound room.

"That is the extremely great granddaughter of the Mona Lisa," Jack said, staring at the screen.

"Hmm..." Sarah took a moment to consider. "How do you think they feel about their ancestor being whored on everything from mouse-mats to dishcloths?"

Jack turned to Sarah. Her gentle smile made him nervous, and he had to steady himself before speaking.

"Are you checking up on me?"

"You're in my café."

"Your café?"

"Yeah. Do you want some coffee?" Sarah turned to the counter and called. "Charlie."

Charlie looked over the counter. He was a middle-aged man with a braided beard hanging from his pointed chin. Sarah held up two fingers in a 'fuck-off' gesture. Charlie raised his thumb.

"You know where that came from?" Jack asked.

"What?"

"That?" Jack held up two fingers.

"Hollywood?"

Jack shook his head. "It was one of those wars between England and France. The French soldiers would cut those two fingers off any of the English archers they captured. So, when the English were running away, they'd go like that." He raised his fingers again. "They still had their fingers."

"Is that true?"

"I don't know. There's no evidence that it's true, but it's a good story."

Charlie brought their coffee. He set the tray down beside Sarah and left with an ugly glance to Jack.

"Does he have a problem with me?" Jack asked.

"Charlie and I go back a few years. When I first moved here, he had a band, and I sang with them a couple of times."

"You were in a band?"

"The Rosenbergers."

"The Rosenbergers? Oh, the spies."

"Buffy ... The Vampire Slayer? Willow Rosenberg? *'She's an ass-kicking Wiccan from Sunnydale.'*"

"Was that one of your songs?"

She shook her head.

"Do you still have a band?"

"No. Do you have anything on?"

"Now? No."

"Well, there's an old picture house, not a movie theatre, a picture house, they show old movies. If you want to kill a few hours?"

"Is this a date?"

"No."

"What's on?"

"There's a double feature on tonight. *Brief Encounter*, and..."

They sat in the back row, Sarah wrapped up in the movie. She had a bucket of popcorn on her lap and a large coke in her seat's cup holder. Beside her, Jack wondered what he was doing there. He began to speak. Sarah snapped, "Shush." She pointed to the screen. "This bit is brilliant." On screen, Dr. Pretorius raised his hands, and smiling like some malignant deity, announced: *The Bride of Frankenstein*.

Jack and Sarah came out of the cinema and walked along the alley to Shoreditch High Street. There were no cabs available, and so they turned towards Liverpool Street Station. Sarah reached into her pocket and turned her telephone on. For a while, they talked about *Brief Encounter*, and the England that demanded Trevor Howard and Celia

Johnson abandon their love in favour of lives that were killing them.

As they passed an off-licence, they saw a couple of kids arguing up ahead. They looked to be about fourteen years of age. They stopped arguing when they noticed the couple who were approaching. One of the kids ducked out of sight. The other looked Sarah up and down as she and Jack passed.

"Sorry, mate?" he called.

When Jack and Sarah did not answer, the kid ran up to them. "Excuse me, Sir."

Jack turned to see him standing, defiant, yet trying to look friendly.

"What's up?" Jack asked.

"Me an' my mate are trying to get some vodka." He nodded back towards the off-licence.

"You think I'm going to buy it for you?"

"I'll pay you." He pulled a twenty-pound note from his pocket.

"Actually," Sarah said, "I fancy some vodka. Back in a minute." She went back to the off-licence while Jack stayed listening to the kid argue his case.

There was no way Jack was buying alcohol for them, when he was in his early teens, a friend, eager to prove his manhood, downed half a bottle of whisky. Soon after, he began to throw up. He collapsed in convulsions on the ground. Jack tried CPR, but his friend was dead within an hour.

It was only when the kids gave up and left that Jack realised how long they had been talking. He walked back to the off-licence and pushed the door, expecting it to open, but his hand slammed against the metal plate and a shock ran up his arm. He tried to look through the front window, but could not get a clear view past the bottles, cans, and posters offering cheap booze. He went back to the door and stood looking at it. A buzzer sounded, and the door was unlocked. Jack slowly pushed it open and stepped inside.

The cashier stood behind a glass-topped counter that ran the length of the shop. He eyed Jack suspiciously.

The tinny sound of the latest hits, re-recorded as wallpaper, accompanied Jack as he walked along behind the furthest aisle. He covered the shop, and turning to the cash register, discovered he was alone.

He called out. A loud crash answered from upstairs. Then a flood of angry obscenities washed that sound away. Jack looked along the counter for an opening but found none. Very carefully, he climbed over the glass counter top. He had just stepped onto the floor when the cashier returned. "Oi! What the fuck are you doing?"

There were twenty feet between them. The cashier looked around, then reached for something under the counter. Jack ran. He grabbed the cashier and slammed him against the wall.

Suddenly Jack was pulled back and up. His backside went through the glass countertop and smashed through the front. His legs dragged through the broken glass and his body twisted as he fell to the floor. He heard his name called, he tried to turn his head, but whoever was on top of him had a solid grip, and all Jack got for his effort was a creak in his neck.

"Do you know him?" the cashier asked.

"Yeah. We were just at the movies."

A voice above Jack spoke, "Sir, I'm a policeman, do you want to press charges? Sir?"

The cashier looked at Sarah. Her eyes pleaded for clemency.

"What does he want? Why did he attack me?" The cashier seemed to be peering at them from a great distance. The world had become far too big, and he could feel the threat of tears. The policeman loosened his grip. Jack looked up at Sarah. She stood at the shop door with a bottle of vodka in her hand.

"Sir?" the policeman asked again. He could feel an

arrest slipping away. The cashier shook his head. The policeman stood up and helped Jack to his feet.

"Would you care to explain what you were doing, sir?"

Sarah, the cashier, and the policeman, all looked at Jack, waiting for his explanation.

"I came in to look for you," Jack said to Sarah.

"Me?"

"You'd been gone a long time. I came in to look for you. He was looking at me kind of suspicious. I didn't think anything of it until I saw the shop was empty.

"Then I heard... I don't know; it sounded like someone was being murdered."

The policeman, suddenly back on duty, turned to the cashier.

"Upstairs," Jack said.

The cashier began to shake. "I, I just, knocked, something over."

"It sounded like someone was being attacked," Jack said. "I was going to check it out when he came back. I thought he was going for a gun."

"This isn't America." The cashier snorted his contempt.

"And what happened upstairs, sir?" the policeman asked.

"I just knocked some stuff over; that's all."

A wry smile appeared on the policeman's face. His twenty years experience gave him a fair idea of what to expect.

"You don't mind if I take a look, do you, sir?"

Reluctantly, the cashier led the procession up the stairs as all four went to investigate. There was nothing out of the ordinary in the first two rooms. In the third, dolls littered the floor: a mass orgy of heroes from the far side of the galaxy. The cashier shrugged his shoulders, embarrassed, and turned a sheepish grin on Sarah.

"Aren't you a little old to be playing with dolls, sir?" the policeman asked.

"They're not dolls," the cashier snapped. He had left his post because he suddenly realised how he could win the vast intergalactic war raging in his bedroom and get back in time to serve the geezer in the shop. Imagining medals and a kiss from the princess, he launched his counter-offensive; then he tripped over a cardboard woman with dangerously large breasts. He fell across the galaxy, sending his soldiers and stratagems flying. The well-ordered battlefield was now a mess. This is why he opposed women in the military.

"Where did you go?" Jack asked. They were walking towards the train station.
"I went to get a lemon." Sarah smiled, but whether she was amused or touched by his concern, Jack could not tell. His own feelings began to trouble him.
"I don't like this business," Jack said, "It's dirty. I'm not used to working like this."
"It'll soon be over."
"Did you at least get a lemon?"
"Oh yes," she said and hooked her arm through his.

Sarah produced a tin of caviar. She opened it, scooped a little onto her finger and put it into her mouth. Jack watched her lips close around her finger and stretch into a satisfied smile as her tongue worked on the caviar. She slowly withdrew her finger from her mouth. She offered the tin to Jack; he looked doubtfully at the dark substance within. It brought back the memory of nightmares about eggs hatching in his stomach and thousands of baby sturgeons swimming about in his blood stream.
"It's a long way from fish eggs that I was raised." The words belonged to his grandfather, and Sarah could hear the lilt of a cod-Irish accent creep into Jack's voice.
"When I was a girl," Sarah said, "my mother would feed me caviar every day. She said it would help me to develop a sophisticated pallet. She insisted I grow up a

An Empire of Silence

properly rounded woman."

Jack stood back and smiled at her body. "Well," he said, "you certainly did that."

"You bastard!" Sarah laughed. Their eyes met, and Jack found himself entertaining thoughts of courtship; long walks in the park; visits to the zoo; the planetarium; chocolates and flowers; days that end with a kiss goodnight on some moonlit doorstep. He leaned in to kiss her. Sarah pulled back. "No."

Jack moved closer. Their lips were a whisper away from each other.

Sarah said, "I'm really sick of one night stands."

Jack's head jerked back. "What?"

Sarah closed her eyes. "I've had sex with a different man almost every night since I've been here."

"Stop," Jack cut in. "Stop right there. We need to get something clear right now."

Sarah looked up, wounded, afraid of the next blow.

Jack continued. "I am not one of your girlfriends. I am not going to be one of your girlfriends. If you don't want to have sex, that's one thing, but do not talk to me like I'm some kind of faggot. You got that?"

"I didn't mean it like that."

What sort of men was she used to? From the evidence of Charlie, the limp wristed rebel at the internet café, she was not used to men at all. But she had held her own in a room full of thugs, expensive thugs, to be sure, but thugs none the less, who, if she had spoken to them as she had spoken to Jack just now, would have knocked her down and raped the bitch. For a moment that thought filled Jack, and he turned away, afraid that he might.

He turned back to her. "Never talk to me like that again," he said.

Sarah looked away, unable to meet his eyes.

"I should go."

"You don't have to go." He hated the thought of her not being there.

Sarah looked at Jack, and he saw a history of damage. Jack's impulse was to hold her, to take her into himself, to save her from the world. He felt that he knew her intimately and that if he could hold onto her, Sarah would bring him things that the flesh he paid for could only withhold. He went to the table, poured two drinks and handed one to Sarah. They moved to the couch and sat for hours, talking more than drinking, laying the foundations for future intimacy.

When Sarah was a child, her father made a point of being there at bedtime. After the Nanny had fed her and washed her and tucked her in, he would read to her: Vasari's Lives, Shakespeare, and the Wall Street Journal. No pre-schooler was ever so well versed in high finance, the Elizabethan Theatre, or the Italian Renaissance. He took her to the stock exchange so she could see 'Animals in their Natural Habitat'. He tried to instil in her the idea that wealth and money are not always the same thing. But when she was two months old, he had waved a hundred dollar bill in her face, "This can get you anything."

To Jack, these slivers of her life were almost inconsequential, even if they were true. Despite his feeling for Sarah, in the back of Jack's mind was the suspicion that she was playing him, that everything he felt was just some kind of romantic nonsense. When Sarah asked about his life, Jack offered his own slivers. He recalled a sitcom in which the head of a standard working-class sitcom household declared *War and Peace* to be the greatest book ever written. When the person he was speaking to said he had never read it, the head of a standard working-class sitcom household said, "Oh no, I haven't read it. I just mean it's great." He pointed to where a hardback copy of *War and Peace* held up one of the legs of the television. The implication that working-class people were too stupid to understand literature stung Jack. Years later, out of some kind of solidarity with 'the people', he checked *War and Peace* out of his local library. He recalled some interesting things about the impossibility of military genius, and he recalled being interested in what Tolstoy had to say about history, although he could no longer recall what those things were. In general, Jack regarded *War and Peace* as more tomb than tome. It was a book in which aristocratic men presented their bald, scented and shining heads to dowager princesses: old maids who, never having married, were now filled with a mania for matchmaking, while speaking French and preparing for war: Soap Opera. Yet it had helped to form his character. Jack decided that he should live his life like Bolkonsky on the battlefield, noticing the sky for the first time. He didn't know what that meant, but it sounded good. He loved Prince André's humanity, even though this is what leads to his death. Sarah laughed at the story, but despite his feelings about *War and Peace*, Jack saw nothing funny in using a book to hold up the leg of a television.

09/An Oasis of Sorrow

Jack awoke alone in bed. Shards of sunlight pierced his eyes. He was almost blind. His body was shaking. His head felt like a ball of electricity. He tried to get up, but the pain was too great. He was too heavy. He tried calling to Sarah but could not form the words. His breath came in short gulps and felt like it was scraping his windpipe. He dragged himself to the side of the bed and pushed his head over the edge. There was a large pool of vomit on the floor. Determined to get up, he pulled his head back and eased one leg over the side of the bed. It fell to the floor, and the momentum pulled his body down. Everything was pain. He tried to get up and collapsed. His head came to rest in the vomit.

Jack's eyes opened. He was on the floor. His head was clear, and he felt completely energized. The smell of vomit came to him, and he began to retch, throwing-up nothing but air. Dry vomit, caked to the side of his face, cracked and tore as Jack lifted his head from the carpet. He wiped it away as best he could and sat on the bed.

How long had he been sitting there? When did he get dressed? He went into the sitting room.

    A splash of red on the carpet: Sarah's shoes. They

stood as if abandoned in mid-stride. *She was still here.* Did they have sex in the end? If so, was it any good? For a moment, the prospect of having failed in bed overtook all other concerns. The bathroom door was ajar. Jack could hear the sound of the shower turned on full.

"Sarah. You want some breakfast? Something for your hangover? Sarah?" Jack pushed open the bathroom door. His eyes closed. His head turned. He stumbled backwards and tripped over his own feet. Pain twisted through Jack's body as he fell, fighting the memory of a greater pain. A word formed in his mouth, parted his lips, but he did not have breath enough to sound the name he loved. He almost cried, but checked himself and got back on his feet.

He took a moment to steady his nerve and went back into the bathroom, forcing himself to look at Sarah. She was slumped, half-naked and lifeless in the bath, her right leg hanging over the edge, her left leg folded beneath itself, leaving her exposed and obscenely vulnerable. Her head flung back, her mouth open as if in the throes of ecstasy. Her right arm twisted behind her back, her left arm lay simply by her side as if in peaceful repose. Her breasts fell away to each side as cold water slammed into her body.

Jack reached in and turned the water off. He lifted her out of the bath and laid her down on the floor. Fighting against the noise in his own mind, Jack listened for a heartbeat. He heard the faint murmur of life in her breast and began pounding down on her heart. He listened again. She was coming back to him. Her eyes snapped open and she jumped up, choking. Her hand grabbed the edge of the bath. She pulled herself up onto her knees. She threw up. When he thought she had finished, Jack began to stand up. Sarah reached out and grabbed his arm. He knelt down beside her, and she was sick again.

When Sarah finished throwing up, Jack helped her into the sitting room and the deep cushions of the couch. He continued through to the bedroom. After a few moments, he returned with an armful of fresh clothes. He stood in the doorway watching Sarah undress, her eyes fixed on the floor. She began to struggle. She stopped. She looked like a child, fighting off something she could not understand.

She searched her arm to find the problem. She began to shake. She was breathing in panic. When Jack moved to help her, she pulled back and sat looking at him with wounded eyes.

"It's caught," he said.

"What?"

"The sleeve of the dress. It's caught."

Sarah looked down at where the sleeve of the dress was caught on her elbow. For a moment she understood nothing, then very carefully, she tugged at the sleeve until it came off. Jack moved, and she jumped, animated by fear, she wrapped her arms around herself and tried to hide. Jack put a pair of jeans and a T-shirt on the couch. He went back to the bedroom and tried to piece together the events since they had returned to the hotel. He wanted to ask what she remembered but decided it could wait. He went into the sitting room. Sarah was still only half dressed and looking around her like some kind of feral child on display at the palace. Suddenly she jumped up, frantically searching her bare arms, "Oh Jesus oh Jesus oh Jesus."

Jack went over to her, calling her name, trying to calm her, but she continued, "Oh Jesus oh Jesus oh Jesus."

He took hold of her. He tried to hold her eyes. He finally smacked her hard across the face. Her head jerked away. She scrambled into a corner of the couch and made herself as small as possible.

She looked at Jack. If she had known him, she would have noticed that the lines around his eyes were a little deeper, his skin was a little paler. If she had known what it looked like, she would have recognised his concern.

"Sarah, what happened?" he whispered.

Sarah continued looking at him, suspicious and ready to strike.

"Sarah?"

"Someone was here," she mumbled.

"In the room?"

She nodded.

"And what happened?"

"He, he injected me," Sarah said. She turned her head away as she was drawn to some internal image. All of her movements slowed to a stop; her attention captured by four letters, blinking on and off. "He injected me."

"What?"

"Someone injected me with something," she said. She waited, looking at Jack, searching for some kind of recognition, anything that would let her know he understood what might have happened.

"I want an AIDS test." Her words came without a hint of emotion. It was a simple statement of fact. No longer the vulnerable child of moments before; someone had threatened her life, and she needed to take action.

Jack and Sarah stood outside the door of a small walk-in surgery. For each of them, embarrassment and nervousness mixed with the memories of previous visits to a clap clinic.

"Come on," Sarah said. She pushed the door open and, reluctantly, they entered the reception. Jack gave their cover story to the receptionist. She gave them a numbered ticket and directed them to the waiting room.

A young child running around a table in the centre of the room held her arms like wings behind her and threw her head back. She lifted each leg with delicate action, becoming airborne for a few seconds before resolutely planting each foot on the floor and taking off again. Sarah smiled at the girl, recalling the ballet lessons of her childhood. She smiled at the girl's mother, who was suddenly embarrassed and felt the need to explain herself.

"She has me run ragged."

The girl, aware that she was being talked about, stopped in her flight and grinned up at her mother.

"Haven't you."

"No. I haven't," the child said. She grinned and took off again.

"How old is she?" Sarah asked.

"Four."

"Four and a half," the girl sang out without stopping.

A single chime sounded, and all heads turned to a monitor on the wall, where the number fourteen flashed in big red figures.

A man sitting by the door looked from the monitor to his ticket. He stood up as the girl came around the corner of the table. She stopped in front of him, breathing heavily and grinning. He smiled at her. The girl turned and ran to her mother. The man gave a short grunt of a laugh and left the waiting room. The mother and daughter were called next.

The number on the monitor changed again. A dark feeling came over Jack and Sarah, their hands snaked out, found each other and squeezed.

They gave their cover story to the Doctor. He examined each of them, and finding nothing wrong, sent them to the nurse on the first floor to give blood samples. They came out of the clinic feeling more nervous than before. There was nothing to do now but await the results.

They took a tube to Baker Street and walked to Regent's Park. They stopped for coffee at the Garden Café and watched people pass by. To the casual observer they were lovers at the end of an affair, both of them wanting it to go on, but knowing whatever they had was lost. Their silence slowly penetrated the surrounding tables and finally Jack and Sarah were alone: an oasis of sorrow in the bright afternoon.

An abandoned newspaper on the next table caught Jack's attention. He reached over and picked it up. He searched the front page, found what he was looking for, and showed the paper to Sarah.

"Look at this." He pointed to the date. Her eyes

widened. The newspaper was dated November 15. They had been unconscious for two days. Of all the questions that raced through Jack's mind, the most pressing was why nobody had found them. If the shower had been running for two days, why had no one come to investigate?

"I don't understand," Sarah said. She asked Jack the questions he had just asked himself. As he listened, without being able to pinpoint exactly why, Jack was sure Sarah was lying. He leaned across the table and whispered "Why would someone inject us with anything?"

"Us?"

Jack waited for Sarah to continue. She felt herself weaken beneath his need for useful information. Should she tell all she knew about the auction? The people behind it? She could no longer look at him. She pushed her chair back and stood up. The chair fell over, and every head in the room turned to their little island. Sarah left the café. Jack, embarrassed by the attention, took out his wallet and opened it. He had only fifty-pound notes. He took one out as a waiter arrived to pick up the chair.

'You said the wrong thing there, mate,' the waiter said.

'Yeah,' Jack said. He gave the waiter a fifty, and followed Sarah.

Outside, Jack scanned the crowd. He spotted Sarah walking quickly towards the Triton Fountain. He caught up and grabbed her arm.

"What the hell's going on?" he demanded.

Sarah snapped her arm away and walked faster. Jack followed, he caught up and matched her pace.

"Sarah?"

Sarah stopped at the fountain. She turned to Jack, hurt and angry that he did not trust her.

"Sarah," he said softly. "If these people are trying to..."

Sarah sat down on the wall. Jack could see his question in the slump of her shoulders, the curve of her back.

"I need to do something," he said. "I need to know what's going on."

Sarah made two attempts to speak before almost whispering, "What do you want me to know?"

Jack sat beside her. "What do you think?" he asked.

"It may have happened because I switched my cell off," Sarah said. As she spoke, Jack listened for any inflection in her voice, watched for any movement that might indicate she was lying.

"What do you mean?"

"I'm supposed to keep my cell phone turned on so they can track the signal. They want to keep an eye on me; they want to know where I am at all times. The other night, when I switched the phone off, they must have come round."

They sat thinking about this; about the implications; about the night they might go to sleep and not wake up in the morning.

Sarah stood up. "This wall is damp," she said. A moment, then they laughed. In the middle of their nightmare, a damp wall seemed absurd.

"There's a guy by the café," Jack said. "He's looking over. It may be nothing, but see if you recognize him."

Sarah scanned the faces of the people hanging about. He looked away, and she saw him.

"I don't recognize him," she said. "He's too far away, but if he is spying on us, he's not very good."

"We'll see," said Jack. "Up here."

They turned towards Queen Mary's Garden, and Sarah noticed the man looking at them. Then she realised he was looking, specifically, at her. He had a strong and very dark presence that was not there a moment ago. She told Jack.

Inside the garden, they sat down and waited. When the young man showed, Jack stood up.

"Hello." Jack reached out to shake hands. On reflex, the young man took Jack's hand, and Jack squeezed.

Confused and frightened, the young man looked to Sarah.

"Well?" Jack asked Sarah. She shook her head. She did

not know him.

Jack squeezed until pain showed in the young man's face. "Why were you watching us?"

"I wasn't watching you." He was shaking. There was cowardice in his voice. Jack felt the young man weaken, and he began to question his own actions. Looking into the young man's terrified eyes, Jack felt suddenly dizzy. He released the hand.

Jack's vision blurred and he staggered. Sarah caught him before he fell. She walked him to a bench and sat him down. When they looked up, the young man was gone.

"Are you OK?" Sarah asked.

"Yeah, I'm fine. I'm fine. Must be the drugs." A poor excuse, but it was the most plausible that he could find. He took a couple of deep breaths. "That house, the house where the authentication happened. Where is it?"

"Why?" Sarah's face froze. She waited.

"I don't like who this is turning me into... There's more to this than a painting," Jack said. "You say we were injected as a warning. What happens next time?"

Jack watched his words work their way through Sarah.

"If somebody has been watching us," he said, "we have to assume they're watching us now. So, unless you've been assigned to me, tell me where that house is. And if you have been assigned to me, what's going to happen once this thing is over? Once you outlive your usefulness?" Again, Jack waited for her to answer.

"Sarah?"

She had moved away from him and isolated herself. He could almost see the space around her. He went over and turned her to face him. There was a confession in Sarah's look that Jack could not quite read, but he understood she was in danger. Jack's common sense told him to walk away, but if he did, would he ever find Sarah beside him again?

"You're right," Sarah said. "There is more going on than the painting. I don't even know if it's real."

"Was the authentication faked?"

"I don't know. I was following a script."

"What about the house? Where is it?"

She stepped away. "Who do you represent? Really?"

Jack almost answered, "I work for the government," but even he did not believe that trite cliché. Instead, he said, "Me. I represent myself. But as to who hired me for this particular job, I really don't know." Even those words felt contrived. He reached out to Sarah.

"Whatever hold these people have on you —"

"You can help," Sarah cut in. There was sarcasm in her voice.

"I don't know. I won't know that until you tell me."

"I don't know," she said.

"Tell me what I want to know or I'm leaving. Now."

Each of them felt echoes of another time; other negotiations; other trusts that had been broken. Each felt the other withdraw a little and, for a moment, each was a continent unto themselves, with only the gathering darkness between them.

"You remember the airfield we took you to. The house is about a mile further on. We loaded you onto the plane and flew around for two hours, then landed in the same place."

"How do I get there?"

10/Moonlight in the Fragrant Air

Jack took a tube to Piccadilly Circus and emerged into rain. He walked around for an hour, working out a plan. He decided to buy a new suit. The clothes he had brought with him from America would be useless for tonight's work. He needed something to make him invisible in the street and help to hide him in the shadows of the house. Eventually, he found a department store that sold discounted clothes. He went in and bought a cheap black suit, (the label claimed the weave was Teflon coated) and a dark blue linen shirt. At a catalogue shop, he bought a gift pack containing a small flashlight and a compass in a metal box.

Back at the Dorchester, Jack took a cold shower and dressed in his new clothes. The prospect of work delighted him, after the last few days, he was himself again. He ordered a plate of ham sandwiches and a pot of coffee, to line his stomach before setting out; a full dinner would have been too heavy.

It was beginning to get dark when Jack left the hotel and climbed into a taxi. They drove around for half an hour, then Jack asked the cabbie to pull in; he paid the fare and got out. He lost himself amongst the commuter crowds on the way to Charring Cross. He took a tube to Waterloo and from there a train to Wye.

In the crush of the outbound train, a forest of arms reached for support as the carriage rocked and sped its way to the Home Counties. Jack stood, half-hidden by a mop of blonde hair that had been teased out until it resembled an afro. From behind this cover, he searched for any pair of eyes that might be searching for him. A familiar face in this crowd spelt danger.

Wave after wave of indistinct chatter and music reached him. The demands of concentration, the close-packed bodies, the smell of perfume and sweat, made Jack nauseous. There were moments when his vision blurred. Every time the train doors opened, he bathed in the merciful breeze. After a few stops, he noticed they were no longer taking on passengers. Soon each station would ease the crush, reuniting families for their brief lives between the office and sleep. It was times like this that Jack was glad not to be part of the world.

A new smell boarded the train, perfumed the air, behind him, in front of him, to the sides. The smell of sex with the perfect woman. Jack felt his sudden erection press against the backside of the woman with the afro. He felt the memory of a slap in the face, and stepped back. He looked at her reflection in the window, from that dark mirror she smiled at him. He relaxed and smiled back. She was about thirty with petite features set in a broad face, a pretty girl-next-door face. She pushed her backside hard against Jack and softly moved, gently teasing his erection. She smiled at his smiling reflection, her eyes dancing with his in the glass, as the light spun gold into her hair.

From behind his evening paper, a middle-aged man nodded at Jack and gave him a 'get in there my son, give her one for me,' smile. Jack ignored him and against his better judgment, enjoyed the distraction. How many others had shared her release from the drudgery of work? He liked the look in her eyes that said, 'This is just a bit of fun. Once I'm gone, I'm gone.' Still, Jack wanted to meet her again, to feel that backside naked against him, to clamp his hands on those breasts, his mouth on hers. Then the train stopped, the door opened and she was gone. With a wink to Jack, the man behind the newspaper also got off the train. Were he and the woman lovers? Jack turned his head and searched the crowd but could not find them.

A few more stops and the train had emptied enough for Jack to get a seat. He took it gratefully, flexing his toes inside the safety boots. He turned his attention to the job. He enjoyed the comfort of knowing there was a problem in front of him, something that would allow him to take action. What did he hope to find at the house? What else was going on?

He looked at his watch; it was coming up on eight. The warmth of the carriage and the train's gentle rocking brought Jack to the edge of sleep. The sound of the other passengers became a pleasant background, broken only by the soft voice announcing each stop. After leaving each station, Jack opened his eyes and looked around, but nobody was interested in him. Then the soft voice called out Wye.

Jack and two others got off the train at a picture postcard station. Jack went into the station café and waited to see if they'd follow. When they didn't, he relaxed and took a seat at the bar.

A boy of about seventeen sat flirting with the barmaid. She looked to be twenty years older than him, which is why he was flirting with her. Jack let them enjoy each other a moment longer. He took in the room. The only other person was an old man who sat nursing his bitter by the empty grate of an older fireplace. He stared into space, regaling an imaginary fire with stories of when he was the signalman.

Jack ordered a cup of coffee. The boy turned to the fucking Yank who was trying to pull his bird, and stripped his teeth in a smile that promised a violent end. The door opened, and a woman came into the café. She sat at a table and pulled a chick-lit novel from her bag. She opened the book and flicked through it until she found where she had left off, then settled down to read. Jack turned back to the bar, smiling as his coffee arrived; he drank it quickly and left. Outside the station was empty. He waited to see if the woman followed. When she didn't, he looked around. In the near distance, village lights reflected stars that city dwellers never see. In the opposite direction, the house stood dark against the night.

Jack started walking towards the house. A couple of cars passed but didn't seem to pay any attention to him. When he came within sight of the house, he left the road. Hidden by trees and hedges, Jack trudged across two fields and was soon staring at an old country manor.

Dirty light burned behind the house. Jack heard the sound of people working. He ducked under cover and continued until the back of the house was completely in view. A man stood by the open top half of a stable door, talking to someone inside. Moments later, he swung the door open, and three men came into the yard. For a while, they stood talking and then the first man locked the stable door. All four climbed into a Range Rover, and Jack watched them drive away. When the lights disappeared from view, he made his move.

He found a small window at the side of the stable. He released the window latch and climbed through, into a small office. He took out his torch and switched it on. Pinned to the wall opposite the desk, he found the racing history of a horse called *Lucky Lad*. Jack tried the desk drawers; they were locked. Two filing cabinets, also locked, moved easily, and Jack was able to pull them forward. He leaned them back against the wall, leaving the underside accessible, then reached under and released the locking mechanism. He opened each drawer: rust, spiders and dusty webs. He pushed the cabinets back against the wall, lining them up as they had been when he entered. He opened the office door and caught the smell of something he could not place, a metallic smell that he enjoyed; the smell of a childhood running wild around the docks of New York. Moonlight in the fragrant air gave the scene a hint of romance. Jack shrugged it off and walked the length of the stable, not knowing what he was looking for. He stopped at the third stall. There was a pattern in the dirt. It did not have the same hard consistency as in the first two stalls. He rechecked to make sure, there was definitely a difference. He cleared away the straw from the floor of the third stall. Six wooden railway sleepers and at least one of them had been recently moved. He put his torch down, picked up a pitchfork and dug it as deeply as possible into the end of the railway sleeper. As the sleeper began to rise, light spilled from his torch into an arms dump beneath.

Jack eased the sleeper back down, replaced the dirt in the crack and packed it tight. There may be answers in the house. He turned his torch off and put it into his pocket. Back into to the office and out through the window.

He turned to the house. The downstairs windows were all barred. The back door was new, solid oak with a Chubb lock. The only way through it was with an axe. Then, on the first floor, he saw his chance. A small window left open a crack. He had come across this type of window before. It locked with a simple latch. He would need something to open it from the outside. He took out his torch, turned it on and cast it around the yard, but found no sign of anything he could use. He unlaced his boots, took them off and stored them in the shadows. He made a noose of the laces and draped it around his neck. He picked up a fistful of fine gravel and rubbed it between his hands. He gripped the drainpipe. It felt secure enough. Hand over hand, he crossed the fifteen or so feet from the ground and arrived at the window. He reached out to inspect it. The timber flaked away in his hand. He swung his bootlace noose down inside the window and hooked the latch, a few gentle tugs and the window dropped open.

Jack climbed inside. His foot almost slipped from the toilet seat into the bowl. He steadied himself and stepped down. He took out his torch and switched it on. The cubicle was the width of the door facing him. He pushed the door. It opened slowly, and he stepped out into a dusty hallway. A quick examination of the floor showed that his were the only footprints. Looking along the hallway, he found a staircase leading down and went to check it out. The third step had an outline of dust gathered around where someone had been sitting. Jack went down the stairs, keeping to the sides of each step and walking on the edges of his feet. He found himself in a large country kitchen. Dirty windows defusing the light, the shadows of bars across the floor, gave the room a ghostly air. Beside the stairs, a large refrigerator buzzed. A dripping tap seemed to mark time, adding urgency to the situation. On Jack's left, the door leading to the rest of the house. He crossed the floor and looked through the keyhole. Faint light spilled from an open doorway. A shadow appeared in the light. It grew into a silhouette that became de Valfierno's assistant stepping into the hall. He was followed by someone Jack did not recognise. A third man came out of the light and closed the door. De Valfierno's assistant spoke to one of the men. He turned towards the kitchen.

Jack looked for somewhere to hide. He heard a hand slap the door. He stood, tense, ready for action. He caught sight of his reflection in the window, and quickly dropped down on his hunkers. The door swung open. It stayed open, but Jack remained tense. He held his breath. Unable to see anything, he listened to the sound of leather on the flagstones as the man walked around the table and checked the back door. The man stopped. Did he know that someone was there? More footsteps led to a soft noise. The room lit up as a huge shadow bent across the opposite wall. The sound of bottles being moved about. Then the fridge door closed and the room returned to darkness. The man left the kitchen, closing the door behind him. Jack waited, breathing softly. Hoods and their sodas, he thought.

"You get one of those for me?" A voice called from

the hallway. There was no response and once again, Jack prepared for action, but no-one came back to the kitchen. Finally, locks opening, the front door slammed and silence.

Jack stepped into the hallway, and over to the door through which the Hoods had come. He closed his eyes and stood listening for any incongruous sound. When he felt the stillness of the house, he opened the door and walked down into darkness. The smell reminded him of a mausoleum he and some friends had broken into when they were kids. He stood on the bottom step, switched his torch on and cast it around. The circle of light leapt like an acrobat: three tier bunk beds, tall metal lockers. A terrible sound in the shadows.

"Sweet Jesus!" He dropped the torch. It hit the step and fell beneath the stairs. The rolling light showed well-fed rats scurry across the floor. Jack looked down at the light; he had to get it back. He tried to think of happy things to make his heart slow down. He undid his belt, took it off and lashed out and the rats. He hunkered down and closed his eyes to clear his mind. He pictured his hand plunging down, grabbing the torch and making it safely home. He opened his eyes, looked at the torch, took a few deep breaths, and did just that before his nerve failed. Trying not to run, and shaking all the way, he went back up to the hallway and shut the door.

There was another set of stairs by the front door. Jack made his way to the top floor, opening doors as he went. A succession of derelict rooms. In some, peeling wallpaper revealed the changing tastes of generations. In others, high wainscoting was scored by sunshine through boarded up windows. In every room, the floors were bare, save for dust and rat droppings. Behind the final door, a flight of stairs climbed to the attic.

Jack entered the vast space now draped in midnight, making a cubist sculpture of cardboard boxes stacked against the gable wall. He went over to inspect them and found the ordinary things he might have found in any attic:

old LP's, photographs, clockwork toys made of tin, comic books and annuals, Eagle, The Dandy, The Man From UNCLE: a childhood packed away for safe keeping, corrupted now by mildew. A little more care and they would have been worth a fortune, as it was they were trash.

"OK, Limey, come on down." It was the same voice that had asked about the soda. Had he come back, or had he been left behind? Jack held still for a heartbeat, and then he heard the heavy thread of the man's shoes as he climbed the stairs. What the hell was going on? Jack moved over to the door, ready for action.

"Come on Limey, we know you're up here, we know you broke into the office, and we know you're nowhere else in the house."

At least he was talking, thought Jack. A truly dangerous man would give no time to prepare. A truly dangerous man would come silently up the stairs, announcing his presence only when he pressed his gun into Jack's back and offered to repay any movement with death. From Jack's position, the only real threat was the word 'we'. The barrel of a .38 Smith and Wesson entered the attic, followed by the finger on the trigger. As soon as Jack saw the wrist, he grabbed it with his left hand and punched down with his right. The gun roared and sent a single bullet through the head of Dan Dare. Jack slammed his fist down again, and the gun fell. With all the force he could muster, Jack spun around and smashed his knee into the man's crotch. A terrifying scream filled the attic as the man grabbed himself and staggered backwards, his face burning red. He tripped and tumbled to the foot of the stairs and was silent. He lay perfectly still just outside the attic door.

Jack picked up the gun and waited, listening. Nobody came. He made his way down the stairs, attentive to all the variables in this new game. No sound disturbed the night, no flash of fire in the darkness. He looked at the gunman and knew it was a corpse. He stepped over the body and continued. He moved along the hall towards the first-floor balcony, the gun at his side, his finger on the trigger, his nerves on the rack, his body coated in sweat.

A flash of gunfire lit up the hall. A window behind Jack shattered in a roar of bullets. Replying with two blind shots, Jack moved to the window to check the drop. The ground looked too far away. A single bullet passed within millimetres of his face. He had three shots left. How many did they have?

Movement below. They were getting into position to come upstairs. Jack fired twice more into the hall. He stepped onto the ledge and jumped as a burst of machine gun fire took his place in the window.

Jack hit the ground; the heel of his left foot dug into the gravel and pain shot through his body. His knees buckled, and he fell forward, sure now that death would follow him down. He turned; they should be there, but the window was empty. He struggled to his feet and hobbled to the ditch. Any moment now, they would catch up with him. He lay in the ditch, waiting.

Above him, Jack heard several people pass by. He looked over the edge of the ditch and saw two men coming from the direction of the stable. As they passed the house, the man on the near side held Jack's boots above his head. Jack looked higher and saw the dark outline of a man standing in the window. He called to the others to return and stepped back into the house.

Jack reviewed his night's work, a weapons dump, and barracks, but no sign of the auction room.

His ankle hurt like a bastard, and he was almost one hundred miles from his hotel suite.

Peter Hopkins – III

Mr. Morris considered himself the next Walt Whitman. Unlike Whitman, he had never written a line of poetry. He worked as a teacher and did his best to inspire his students. If you asked how he did this, he would have answered, "My vibrational frequency is in tune with the essence of pure poetry. This eliminates the need actually to write the damn stuff. *I am poetry.*" However, nobody did ask, and in his heart, Mr. Morris bemoaned the fact that he was condemned to a life in the service of morons.

He had been hired to teach English at a time when the school was grossly underfunded, and now they could not get rid of him.

Unfortunately for Peter, Mr. Morris also subscribed to *The UniVerse*. He took it as confirmation of his own genius that one of his students should have something accepted for publication, so it was with considerable pride that he made his announcement. He relished the sound of applause. It took a few seconds to realise the sound was only in his mind. The classroom was silent.

Some of his classmates looked at Peter, no longer sure what to think of him. Of the thirty students in the class, there were fourteen closet poets. Some of them now felt trapped by fear of exposure. One of them tried to escape by mumbling "faggot." The word unleashed a squall of jeers and laughter. Mr. Morris blamed Peter for this affront to his dignity and stood watching the young boy crumble beneath the abuse.

When he became afraid to go to school, after being beaten up while the coach turned a blind eye, it was sheer bloody-mindedness that saved Peter from suicide. He returned to school and punched the first boy to call him a fag.

When his next poem was published, Peter brought a copy of the magazine into school and put it before Mr. Morris.

"Where's yours?" Peter demanded.

The hard men of the class fell silent. However much they ran their teachers down and cursed them; they did it behind their backs; nobody spoke to a teacher like this. That Peter did so now proved his homosexuality in the minds of his classmates. He was a fag trying to cover.

Peter withdrew into himself and settled down to work, to get away from these people. He joined the football team, just in case his grades were not good enough. He hated football, but it might get him into college and away from here.

Then he learned of the Whitely scholarship

11/Rubicon

Jack shifted comfortably and felt a growing sensation of warmth that made him want to stay where he was forever. He opened his eyes and found himself in a large bed. He propped himself up on the pillows to take in the room. Directly across from the bed, a large window full of clouds. To his left, a few logs snapped and burned in an Empire fireplace. The furniture was also Empire: a dresser drawer, chairs and a wardrobe. A crystal chandelier hung from the centre of a large rosetta on the ceiling. To his right, double doors led to the rest of the apartment.

Jack threw back the bedclothes and only then discovered he was wearing silk pyjamas. His injured foot had been bandaged. He swung his legs off the bed and onto the floor to test his foot. It felt a little tender. He stood up, put more weight on the foot. He took a step. Another. He stopped. He waited for the pain to arrive. He took another step. Still no pain. He went to the bedroom door and listened. Voices in Spanish. He looked through the keyhole and saw fire. He stood up and stepped gently to the window. The view was of bogland in every direction. There were stretches of wire fence scattered throughout the Bog. None of them connected, but taken together, they gave the impression of a macabre dressage course.

Jack opened the window. The outside wall was smooth and the window ledge so small it might have been an afterthought. He wanted to jump, but his foot rebelled.

He went to the wardrobe and opened the door. His suit, freshly laundered, hung above a new pair of shoes. He took the suit down and checked the pockets. They were empty, and in that he found comfort. It was the first thing since opening his eyes that made sense. He dressed and went to the bedroom door. He listened for a moment then slowly turned the handle.

He had opened the door only a few millimetres when he heard the voice, "Welcome back."

Jack came fully into the room and looked to where Masterson sat in a corner with a book in his lap. Two men by the fire turned to Jack. One was a South American Indian. The other was the kid who had been in Regent's Park.

"It's OK, Jack," Masterson said. "I'm not the villain of the piece." He smiled. "Give me a moment." He put the book aside and spoke to the men by the fire. They laughed and left the room.

Masterson caught Jack looking at the book, *Rubicon, A History of the Roman Republic,* by Tom Holland. Masterson held up the book. "Do you know it?" he asked. Jack nodded.

"Of course, ours is an empire of silence," Masterson said. "And we will do whatever it takes to keep it that way. Did you know that even before 9/11, Bush was sending memos to Blair, speculating as to how they could provoke Saddam into doing anything that could be used to justify an invasion? Saddam had decided to sell oil in Euros. In the end, of course, they just falsified the evidence.

"I wonder ... would that be Democracy Inaction?" He laughed. "All of this to maintain our empire. Still, the oil will run out, the old men will die, and no-one who counts will care."

"Really?"

"Yes, Jack. Really. As long as the government is in debt to men like Tom Whitely. You know, when Joe Kennedy was buying the presidency for his son, he didn't just do a deal with the Mafia. Tom Whitely made it clear that anyone who did not vote for Kennedy would lose his job. How was he going to find out? Nixon should have won that election. Of course, we should probably thank our lucky stars that he did not.

"Do you believe in lucky stars, Jack?"

Jack did not answer. While Masterson spoke, Jack poured a drink and sat in one of the chairs by the fire. At the mention of Kennedy's name, Jack recalled his own grudge. He had never forgiven the President for the Vietnam War. Although the war did not properly start until after Kennedy's death, he had initiated America's involvement, and although he wanted to bring the troops home, he was happy to wait until after he was re-elected. For Jack, this always came down to the human question: how many people was JFK prepared to kill in order to win an election?

On his second tour of duty in Vietnam, unable to deal with his involvement in the massacre of a village, occupied only by the very old and the very young, all of them unarmed, Jack's father became addicted to heroin. He brought his addiction home and after his divorce became increasingly dependent on the drug.

A nine-year-old boy stands outside the front door of a seven-floor walk-up. He begins to breathe deeply, filling and emptying his lungs with each breath; fighting the stink that has already started to rise in his mind. He takes a final look around to make sure there is no one he recognizes. People with nothing to do are sitting on stoops, sweltering in the New York summer. From somewhere further down the block comes the sound of what, in a few years time, will be called Rap. The boy can see no sign of anyone who might report him and deprive him of one of the few pleasures of his life. When he satisfies himself that the coast is clear, he takes a final breath, then, covering his mouth with the palm of his hand, he pinches his nose against the stink, pushes the door open and enters the building.

"You know me," a voice erupts from a pile of blankets in the hallway. The blankets begin to move and from beneath, yellow eyes with pinprick pupils bore into the boy, looking through him and past him. Broken lips part but now the voice is so devoid of hope that the boy almost starts crying.

"You know me."

The face retreats beneath the blankets, but the voice continues, "You know me. You know me. You know me."

With his lungs burning, the boy steps as quietly as he can past the blankets. Once he is clear, he begins to run, charging the stairs two steps at a time. Walking along the landing, the smell overpowers him. The building always smells like a sewer, but this is worse. It is unlike anything he has ever smelled before. He gags and almost throws up. Somewhere in his mind, he wonders how they can live like this; animals would have more sense.

He pushes open the door to his father's room and stops. His father's face is frozen in a look of pained ecstasy; thin lips stretched to the limit; cloudy eyes look directly at the boy and hold him. He feels a trickle of piss run down his leg. His eyes wander to the holes in his father's body, from where maggots seem to ooze like puss from a boil. In the dead man's left arm, a half-depressed syringe stands upright, casting a shadow, marking the time at 4p.m.

"Jack?"

"Hmm?" Jack returned to the room.

Masterson smiled. Something about him had changed. Whatever it was, the old man was even more grotesque than Jack remembered.

"I said, 'Do you have anything to report?'"

Before Jack could answer, the apartment door opened and the kid returned.

"Well?" Masterson asked.

The kid nodded. He went over to the drinks table and picked up a bottle of water. He opened it and drank.

"Jack, you've met Douglas." Masterson gestured to the kid. Douglas stared at Jack. Masterson put the book away and getting up, sent Douglas to get Jack's things. As he passed the table, Masterson picked up the decanter of whisky and a glass. He crossed the floor and sat in the chair opposite Jack.

"Let's get down to business."

While Masterson poured a drink, Douglas returned with Jack's things. He put them down on Masterson's side table and withdrew to a corner of the room.

Jack reached across to the table; he picked up and inspected, first the wallet, then the metal box; each was exactly as it should be. He put them into his pocket.

"Where are we?" Jack asked.

"Devon. I presume you had a look outside. That romantic wilderness is Dartmoor. You know it?" The question was in response to the look of recognition from Jack.

"Only from Sherlock Holmes."

"Ah, the great detective! Well you were, detected, unconscious in a ditch a few miles outside the village of Wye. By a mailman, believe it or not. He delivered you to the local police station. The police checked your identity and contacted the embassy, and the embassy contacted me."

"When did all this happen?"

"You were brought here at about five o'clock this morning. You're supposed to be in the hospital."

Listening to this, Jack realised what it was about Masterson that had changed. There was a new nose in the centre of the old man's face; subtly different, just enough to throw people off balance. It might still be tender; a useful thing to know if Jack had to hit him.

"Don't worry Jack. We have taken care of the police.

You will not have to answer any questions. Douglas will take you back to London after we've had our little chat."

Jack looked across at Douglas, who was now sitting in the chair his boss had vacated. How many hours to London?

"I'll walk," Jack said.

Masterson laughed. "Well, tell me, what has happened since our last meeting? Have you seen the painting? Is it real?"

Jack searched Masterson's face for any indication of what was wanted, but the too-smooth skin showed no concern; the soulless eyes offered no clues. Jack considered telling him about his research into de Valfierno, but... no.

"I have seen a copy of the painting being authenticated. Whether it's genuine or not –" Jack spread out his open palms to indicate his doubt.

Masterson nodded slowly. He looked into Jack's eyes. Each man waited for the other to surrender.

Jack's stomach broke the tension. He remembered he had eaten nothing but sandwiches for the last few days. He promised himself a hot meal when he got back to London. Masterson smiled. He sent Douglas to get some food.

"What's this all about?" Jack asked.

"I'm sorry Jack, that's an official secret."

Masterson drank his whisky and put the glass down. He relaxed back into the chair and folded his arms across his belly. The barest hint of a smile stretched his mouth, and a sparkle, that could have meant anything, came to his eyes. He let Jack sit there weighing up the odds of getting out alive.

"You want to be a lawman, Jack," he said, "Are you sure you want to do that? You would have to disclose all of your, ill-gotten gains."

"You offered me immunity."

"That only goes so far. What about," then Masterson named the country, the city, the street and the bank in

South America where Jack kept his money. He named the exact amount of money held there and the dates of each deposit. Then, as if he were walking through it, Masterson described Jack's South American penthouse. The book, *Rubicon*, had come from Jack's library. Jack tried to play it cool, but he was afraid. Twice now, Masterson had demonstrated how vulnerable Jack really was. The sense of invasion stung and gave him an understanding of what his own victims must have felt. Jack had never known this feeling before. He sent up a silent prayer that he never would again.

"Did you think we met by coincidence? Jack, we own that country. We bought it back in fifty-five. The whole point of that country is so that people like you will keep your money there. Then, when we have some use for you, we know how to find you."

Douglas returned with a plate of sandwiches and put it on the table. But on learning that he had been burgled, Jack found his appetite was also missing.

"Are you sure?" Masterson asked.

Douglas removed the sandwiches and the whisky. He replaced them with a stack of photographs.

"Recognise someone," he ordered.

Jack picked up the photographs and scanned them. He dropped each picture onto the table when he'd finished with it. Finally his hands were empty.

'No,' he said. He leaned back in his chair.

Throughout this, Masterson sat gazing into the fire, letting his protégé handle the details.

Douglas picked up one of the photographs. He held a magnifying glass to it and pointed out the people he wanted Jack to recognise. Jack recognised Sarah; she was sitting at the café where they first met. She looked like a little girl, trying to hide.

"Her name is Sarah James," Douglas said. "Poor little rich girl. But you know that already."

"No," said Jack, "I don't know her at all."

"This isn't a romance novel," Masterson said, still looking into the fire. His voice was full of pain.

Douglas looked at him a moment and then turned back to his work. He moved the magnifying glass over the image of a man in the photograph.

"Who's he?" Jack asked.

"He deals in futures. Countries, not corn. Here," He handed Jack another photograph. It was blurred but familiar. The image developed in Jack's mind and became the man who had been in the doctor's waiting room: the man in grey.

"He's her boss," Douglas said.

Jack tightened his fist, and he had to kill the urge to punch Douglas in the face.

"The contract," Masterson said. Douglas left the room.

Masterson continued, "Somebody's going to be moving a lot of money around. Hundreds of millions of dollars. Jack, we need to find out who that is. Unfortunately, we live in a world of transparency: The Illusion of Honesty."

Douglas returned with the contract and put it down in front of Jack.

Masterson held out a pen. "Sign it."

Jack signed the contract.

"OK," said Masterson, "as you know, we bought that country in fifty-five. Now it's time for them to become a democracy. There will be elections next month. The first time these people have ever had democratic elections."

"That's not true," Jack said. "They had an election in fifty-five. But they elected the wrong president. He was a Marxist, wasn't he? There was a coup the day after he was elected."

Masterson smiled. "You know your history. Well, never mind. The point is, it is happening again. The gentleman that was here when you woke up, he may be the new president. He grew up in the barrios. The people want him. We would like to see that they get him."

12/Lost Horizon

Jack prowled his hotel suite, feeling like an outcast in his own life.

After twenty miles of silence, Jack asked Douglas to drop him at the nearest train station. Douglas refused; his orders were to make sure Jack got safely back to London.

"In that case," said Jack, "pull in up here. It's going to be a long drive." He indicated a filling station on the outskirts of a small town. Douglas ignored him.

"I need coffee," Jack added.

Without a word, Douglas turned into the forecourt and pulled up in front of the pumps. He turned the engine off and got out of the car. Jack went to get some coffee. When he came out of the shop, he said goodbye to Douglas and started walking towards the town. Glancing sideways from time to time, he saw Douglas following in the car. He followed Jack into the train station, onto the train to London, and took a seat beside him.

For a while, as he watched the occasional house become a village, and villages become towns, Jack thought of nothing but food. He considered ordering something on the train, but changed his mind when he thought about it sitting in a cold-room for God knows how long. He was purposely putting off the thought of her. He felt betrayed, although treachery was her job, as it was his now, he had expected more. But what right had he to expect more? If she looked different; if she looked different, he would have painted her a whore.

When they arrived in London, Douglas went to find the train for his return journey. Jack went to the nearest diner and ordered a bean breakfast. He devoured the meal, not thinking about anything at all.

There were no messages waiting at the Dorchester, although Sarah had called twice. Jack went into the bar and ordered a double Tullamore Dew on the rocks. He sat there for almost an hour nursing his drink, thankful that nobody bothered him. He wondered if Sarah would call, and this became the expectation that she should. As time passed and people were paged, Jack began to worry that his name was not being called. By degrees, his concern degenerated into fear for Sarah's safety.

Now, in his hotel suite, pursued by his longing, Jack prowled through the elegant jungle that surrounded him and spread out beneath his feet. Every movement in the hall outside was his hope that Sarah was alive and safe. Every sound that passed on its way brought her closer to death. "Bitch," he spat. Had he killed her? Jack could see the assassin's hand clamped over her mouth, the finger and thumb pinch her nose closed. He could see her struggle as she was bundled into the back of some grotty van. He could see her body broken until her answers satisfied. Then what? A swift murder? Hours of fun? The brutality of the image exercised itself on Jack's soul until he felt an overpowering need to escape the evil influence.

Jack went hunting down side streets, searching for a bookshop/café, the sort of place where he could find dog-eared copies of out of print books.

He found a shop called *Hey, What You Reading For?* and went inside. A narrow counter ran along the front window where a few people sat reading and drinking coffee. The bookshelves reached from floor to ceiling and were filled with whatever sort of book anyone might want, and the smell, that beautiful old bookshop smell. Jack took a moment to enjoy the smell of the shop, to let that fragrance fill him up, settle into his bones and flush out the melancholy. New books and old, coffee, muffins and scones, apples, oranges and bananas, all of these smells came to Jack and rescued him.

He loved white lines along the spines of books. He wondered about the lives they had passed through. There were no careful owners here. He walked between the shelves, reading titles and authors. *The Penguin Complete Sherlock Holmes*, by Sir Arthur Conan Doyle; *The Ancestor's Tale*, by Richard Dawkins; *The Afternoon of a Writer*, by Peter Handke; *How to Make Love to a Negro*, by Danny Laferriere; *You Only Live Twice*, by Ian Fleming; *Last Exit to Brooklyn*, by Hubert Selby jr.; *Afterglow of Creation*, by Marcus Chown.

Jack stopped; he picked *Afterglow of Creation* from the shelf. He turned the book over. On the back cover, he found a picture of a mathematical graph describing a wave. Beneath this was the legend 'DECODING THE MESSAGE FROM THE BEGINNING OF TIME'. Jack recalled a newspaper headline: *Science Proves the Existence of God.* A local community leader who liked to trumpet his Christian values went on television one night to announce the death of science. "Science," he claimed, "has finally made itself irrelevant." The following evening's paper carried a rebuttal from a woman who claimed "I am a Christian and a Scientist." She wrote that scientists had found radiation left over from the big bang. This did not prove the existence of God, and proving the existence of God was nothing to celebrate. Faith was a compact with a supernatural being, a promise of support for the tough times and eternal life for those who live by love. This means the church is damned. If you prove the existence of God, faith becomes unnecessary, but lawyers become vital, and that, she argued, was unacceptable. She finished her piece by riffing on Lou Reed, *'You're going to reap what's in your soul.'* Within hours of the paper hitting the streets, a

Christian Science reading room was firebombed. To Jack, the existence or non-existence of God was academic. However, the riff had struck a chord. Recalling it now, he found himself riffing on John Lennon, *'God is a conscript, by which we misjudge ourselves.'*

Moving along, Jack found an old copy of *Lost Horizon*, by James Hilton. Jack loved this story of the hidden valley. It was the first book he had ever read for his own enjoyment. He took this and *Afterglow of Creation* to the cash register. He paid for the books and bought a cup of coffee, then took a seat at the window, where he opened *Lost Horizon* and travelled to Shangri-la, until a soft voice called him back. He looked up from the book to see a pink-haired waif with flier in her hand.

"Protest tonight," she repeated.

Jack took a flier to get rid of her. "Thank you," he said.

When she heard Jack's accent, the girl tried to take the flier away, but he moved it out of her reach and scanned it.

"Why are you going to burn my country's flag?"

"You started this war." Her voice was suddenly aggressive.

"Start a war?" Jack asked. "I hate to break it to you sweetheart, but I wasn't even consulted."

Her forehead creased like a baby's and for a few seconds she seemed to be a lifetime away from the anger in her fist.

Jack continued, "You've got this all wrong. There are millions of people across America who display the flag; or wear a flag pin on their lapel, but who don't support the war. They might even support you if you didn't burn the flag.

"You see, the only thing you'll really accomplish by burning the flag is to distract attention away from where it needs to be. The people you think you're protesting really don't give a damn about democracy. If they did, they wouldn't be in office. You burning the flag gives them an excuse to paint you as the enemy. Some of the people who might have supported you will believe them. Some of those people will start to get the idea that this is a just war. Do you understand?

"You should also consider your own country; your country is in this war by choice. Your leaders are as guilty as mine. If you really believe that burning a flag will serve any kind of beneficial purpose, then you have to burn your own country's flag before you burn mine."

Burning her own country's flag had never occurred to her. Now that it was proposed she was horrified. Some deep-seated race memory nagged at her that Britain was somehow above something. Britain had given parliamentary democracy to the world. Yes, her country had done terrible things in the name of Empire, but she had not done those things. Her boyfriend was Pakistani. (In fact, he came from Colchester, and his family had emigrated from India.) She just wanted everyone to be happy. There was no room in her philosophy for the Union Jack in flames. She stood as if trapped in some kind of feedback loop.

Jack had a picture of her life, a respectable middle-class world to which she would return when she finished rebelling. Then she spoke, and the certainties Jack had formed about her fell asunder.

"My brother was killed over there."

"Miriam?" Her head turned, and her face relaxed at the sight of her rescue.

"Come on," he said, "we've got the whole street to do."

"He wants us to burn the flag," Miriam jerked her thumb towards Jack.

"Really?"

"No," said Jack "I don't believe in burning the flag. But if you do, then you should burn your own flag first. You're in this thing just as much as we are."

"Ahh." Miriam's rescue nodded and smiled with the understanding of someone trying to pacify a stupid child.

"Come on, Miriam."

The two of them left.

Jack noticed his coffee, half-full and undrinkable. He took it to the counter and bought another.

"Sorry about that." The shop assistant nodded towards the door.

"No apology necessary," Jack replied. Miriam's confusion and her saviour's contempt had given Jack the measure of them both. To Miriam, the demonstration, the flag burning, was an emotional response. To her saviour, it was an opportunity for political advancement, either within or without the system.

Jack went back to his window seat. He soon forgot the incident and the coffee as he returned to the Valley of the Blue Moon. He did not notice the lights come on; people pass by on their way out of the shop. A voice beside him signalled these changes.

"Sorry sir, I have to close up."

"Hmm?" Jack looked up from the book. He became aware of his surroundings. His reflection in the window looked as though it belonged to somebody else. He turned to the shop assistant, "Wow," Jack said, "I didn't realise."

"Good book."

Jack picked up the flier. "What would Conway make of all this?"

The shop assistant shrugged his shoulders; he had no idea who Conway was. Jack folded the flier into the book, picked up *Afterglow of Creation*, and left the shop.

Jack's return from Shangri-La brought Sarah back to him. Try as he might to lose her on the way, she had haunted his travels, and now her presence filled his mind. As he walked he felt the crowd grow thicker, and he found himself at the demonstration.

Jack made his way to the top of Trafalgar Square to get a better view. Riot police watched for anyone who might be planning to re-enact the famous battle. All down

Whitehall, skulls among the faces, some with lighted candles, floating in darkness, as if the river had given up its dead. The candles, the faces, the painted skulls, seemed to flicker and spark, moving with the movement of the thing they had become; a tide that seemed to flow forever onwards, aflame with hope and death. How many were there in hope? How many in death? How many there to get laid? How many to fight the police? How many to regale their mates in the pub? How many to network? How many to challenge the next Yank they met? How many simply had nothing better to do?

"Would you like a candle, sir?" There was a welcome in the voice. Jack turned to find a smiling bearded Texan holding out a box of candles.

"What are they for?" Jack asked.

"Hey, is that Boston. Well, we're not going to have a tea party but you're welcome to join us."

"For what?"

"For the vigil." He pointed to the crowd. "You're not here for the vigil?"

"I was just passing. What's it all about, anyway?"

"We just want to acknowledge the civilians that have been killed in this war. You know? The news tells us about the soldiers, and we shouldn't forget them. But some estimates put the civilian death toll at between thirty and one hundred thousand souls. We never seem to hear about them. So, my wife and I, she's English, we organised this, just to remind people. I mean," anger entered his voice, "in any conflict, there's going to be, so-called, 'collateral damage', but how do you kill between thirty and one hundred thousand civilians unless you really don't give a damn?

"Y'know? Some of our boys are sent on raids based on information that's been paid for, either with hard currency or with torture. Only a half-wit trusts information like that. The boys are sent in, they can end up killing God knows how many innocent people just to get one guy, and for all anyone knows, that guy was fingered for revenge."

The Texan took a breath, his face flushed. He wanted to hit somebody.

"I saw on TV, some cop show, this guy saying, "WMD, sometimes we get it wrong." As if that's an excuse. We didn't get it wrong. And Bush, "God told me to invade Iraq", God didn't tell him do it. He did it because he's a coward and a criminal. He's a man who spent his whole life abdicating his responsibilities. He used to blame everything on alcohol, now he blames everything on God. And you know the worst thing? Someday he's gonna be seen as a great president.

"I'm sorry man. The whole thing just pisses me off. We send our children off to die. Some of them come home, and the good ones have to live with it, and the bad ones, well, there wouldn't be any bad soldiers if it wasn't at least tolerated at higher levels."

The two men stood looking at each other. The Texan seemed to want a reply. He was acutely aware of the soft candle in his hand. He held it out again. In his pocket, Jack could feel the flier sticking out of his copy of *Lost Horizon*. A strain came to the Texan's eyes. The anger in his voice gave way to sorrow. "But the ordinary folks are still dead."

Jack thought about showing him the flier, but if the Texan had organised the flag burning then Jack's protest would be worthless. If the Texan was not involved, Jack did not want to risk the police.

"No," he said, "I'm sorry. Rough day."

"I've had those, buddy." The Texan softened. "Tell you what, meet me back here afterwards. My wife cooks the best Irish stew you ever tasted. It's about all you can do with the meat over here." He laughed a big joyous laugh that lightened Jack's mood, where ordinarily he would have been irritated. "Come and have dinner with me and my wife. It'll take your mind off it."

"Thank you." Jack took a candle.

"OK," the Texan said, "I'll see you later." The two

men nodded to each other. The Texan walked on, stopping to offer candles to people as he passed. Once the Texan was out of sight, Jack started walking towards Park Lane.

Jack was alive, and that was wrong. It was only his trip to Shangri-la that had made room for this happy doubt. Last night people had been shooting at him, spraying bullets, and missing, hundreds of rounds of ammunition emptied into the walls and even into the window while he was standing there. What odds would Vegas give for his survival in those circumstances? Yet here he was, walking through the streets of London on a crisp November night. The only evidence of his adventure was the vague throbbing in his ankle. His survival suggested that those who had been squeezing the triggers, or those who had given the orders, wanted him out of that house alive.

When he got back to the Dorchester, Jack checked to see if there were any messages. The receptionist gave him a small envelope, inside was a note that simply read: A drink. He went to the bar and looked around without recognising anyone. He took a seat at the bar, ordered a bottle of Guinness Extra Stout and sat drinking, waiting for someone to recognize him. When no one did, he went up to his suite, took his jacket off and threw it over the back of the couch, then opened the French windows.

He went to the bathroom and turned the shower on. He had just finished undressing when the telephone rang. It was Sarah. The sound of her voice swelled Jack's heart, but she had questions to answer. After the call, Jack went back to the bathroom and turned the shower off. He dressed quickly and stood in the sitting room, watching the door, waiting for her knock.

Jack opened the door to disappointment. He had hoped to find innocence in her eyes, but the sight of Sarah did nothing to dispel his doubts. Did something show in his face? Sarah's expression said so as she entered the room.

"Did you find anything?" she asked.

"Yeah." Jack closed the door. He stood for a few seconds with his hand on the handle. He took a breath and turned to face her.

"When we were at the Doctor's, remember? There was a guy in the waiting room."

"Oh, I've put that whole episode out of my mind."

"Well re-run it now."

"Jack?"

"Don't."

Sarah hesitated. "I should go." She moved towards the door. Jack reached out and took her hand. He pulled her to him, twisting her arm up behind her back. With his other hand, he covered her mouth. "You're not leaving this room until I find out who he is."

Sarah stopped struggling. There was the pain Jack had seen in her before. He took his hand away from her mouth.

"You can ask me what you like once I've decided you're telling the truth," Jack said. He released her.

Sarah stepped away and took her jacket off. She turned away and undid her dress, letting it fall to reveal long and short scars across the small of her back. Although none appeared to be recent, the scars cut across each other in painful witness to years of torture.

"I had to hold a chair above my head while he questioned me. Whenever the chair started to slip, he hit me."

This new evidence entirely changed her in Jack's eyes. He searched for the right words, but all he found seemed inadequate. He moved towards Sarah to help put her dress back up. She shrugged him off and moved away.

"He beats you until you enjoy it. Then he stops and moves on to something else." Sarah pulled her dress up and fastened it.

"Why you?" Jack asked. "Sarah?"

"He wanted to recruit me. He's with Homeland

Security."

"Why me?"

She took a long time to answer. Long enough to make something up? Her voice, her body, her eyes, offered no clue.

"I spent two years infiltrating an organization called Alpha-Omega, we gave them that name. After the fall of the Soviet Union, they were the main importers of heroin into Eastern Europe. They brought it in through Prague. It was easy then; everything was for sale. It was said that the beauty of Prague is that Kafka is being whored with greater passion than the women who work Wenceslas Square. The standard fine was three hundred koruna; the standard bribe was one hundred. If the cops stopped you, they asked for a bribe. Anyway, five years ago they stopped altogether, Alpha-Omega, just disappeared off the map. This was around the same time that talk of the Mona Lisa being a fake started to gain some ground. Somebody credible was fuelling these rumours. Then, about two years ago, there were rumblings that Alpha-Omega were back.

"The next thing I knew, I was being sent around the world to contact anyone who might be interested in buying the Mona Lisa. You were the only one I hadn't personally made contact with. So I was assigned to you to find out who you represented."

While Sarah had been speaking, Jack stood where she had shrugged him off. Now he went to the couch and sat down. Sarah took the chair opposite. They sat in silence for a few minutes, sizing each other up; then Jack spoke.

"Is this room bugged?"

"Yes."

"Then why did you tell me what you just did?"

There was an appeal in her eyes that his heart could not ignore. He felt weak, and his head began to swim with the fear of losing himself in his own emotions. When he spoke, his words felt inadequate but he did not know what else to say.

"What's going to happen to you?" he asked.

"I don't know. He'll probably hand me over to the police."

Jack's face asked the question.

Sarah answered, "I used to be a forger."

"How much do you know about what he gets up to?"

"I only know what I need to know."

"Would it be worth his while having you killed?"

Again the silence. Again it was broken by Jack. "Will he be coming after me?"

"Probably, but only to get the people behind you."

"Do they know where the authentication happened?"

"Yes."

"Did you tell them I was going back there?"

"I had to. That kid in the park."

"Was he one of them?"

"There's no way of knowing."

If Sarah was lying, her performance was masterful. Jack relaxed. If they were going to get him, they would get him.

"OK," he said. "I think we're on the same side. I was sent here by a guy called George Masterson. He says he's a government man. They're investigating the sale. I don't believe him, but I'm supposed to bid for the painting."

Jack and Sarah sat, each embraced by the sort of tactile silence one sometimes feels when one is alone.

"This is no good," Sarah said.

"I know."

"I'm sorry." Sarah got up to leave. Jack followed her to the door and opened it. Sarah reached up and kissed him, then whispered, "Meet me in the park tomorrow."

When Jack closed the door on Sarah, he felt the air thicken. The world filled up with her presence. He went to the bathroom and turned the shower on; he threw off his clothes, stepped beneath the warm water and masturbated her out of his system.

13/The Mechanic

Sarah cast some bread upon the water and a swan moved towards her. A young boy, about four years of age, noticed this and turned with disgust to the old woman who had lured his property away from him. When Sarah caught the child looking at her, she pulled a bread roll from her bag, crushed it in her hand to soften the crust and tossed it over to him. The bread roll landed almost at his feet and in payment, he offered Sarah a look of contempt that said he was above the menial task of picking things up. He screamed at his nanny. She picked up the bread roll, ripped it to pieces and threw them to the swans. The boy turned in triumph to Sarah, 'Your turn'. Sarah smiled; she was thinking of all the beatings this little shit will receive throughout his life. She was wrong. Apart of Eton, where a future Prime Minister will bugger and beat him on a regular basis, no one will ever lay a finger on this future First Lord of the Admiralty. When he receives his instructions from the future Prime Minister, the future First Lord of the Admiralty will be told, "I'm not a queer, but I am going to fuck you, and you mustn't think that I do this for sexual pleasure. I do this because you're a cunt."

Sarah tore a piece of bread from the roll in her hand; she held it at arm's length, between her thumb and forefinger, over the water. A swan approached, titled its head towards her, quickly straightened its neck as it opened its beak, snatched the offered food and withdrew.

Jack watched this exchange from across the park. He had been there for an hour during which time Sarah was alone. Jack had watched her while she sat in the café working on a crossword puzzle and drinking coffee. He had watched her dispatch, with a few words, an amorous skinhead. When the skinhead left the café, he had his arm in matey fashion around the shoulder of a fey looking hippy.

Jack approached Sarah, confident that for now, at least, her bosses would not molest him.

He stood a few feet from her. "Well, I'm here."

The smile Sarah expected would leap to her lips never appeared. The perfunctory edge to Jack's voice had pushed it back down. She had envisioned their meeting differently; when Jack arrived, she was going to ease into things by telling him about the swans she used to feed when she was a little girl; (she had deliberately chosen the phrase, 'a little girl'). Huge graceful birds that, her father told her, could break her neck if they wanted, would come and take bread out of her hands.

Jack had also planned a different meeting. When he saw Sarah with the swans, he tried to recall the story of the *Children of Lir*, from Irish mythology: children, charmed to spend eternity as swans, except at night, when they would retake human form. He put this trinket aside and instead offered an agitated, "Well, I'm here." He regretted the harshness in his voice, but he continued. "What do you want?"

Sarah walked to a bench and sat down. She looked up at Jack, then looked away. Her fingers tore at the bread in her hands and tossed it to a gathering flock of pigeons at her feet. She noticed what she was doing and threw the last of the bread to the swans. The pigeons took flight; a blizzard of wings. Sarah joined her hands, she compared her thumbs.

"When I came to your hotel room last night," Sarah began. She stopped, uncertain where this would lead. She struggled to recall something, and then continued. "After you left me here the other day, I started thinking about what had happened, and," she lifted her eyes to his, not pleading but asking for help. "I know you have –"

"I have connections," Jack cut her off. He sat down; taking her in, hoping against hope she was not doing likewise to him. "I know people who can help." He stopped, wondering if he should tell her. He finally decided she had a right to know, "But they're just as lightly to sell you into slavery," he said.

"What?"

"If you want to disappear that's a risk you'll have to take. Everything that ties you to who you are now, all of that has to go. There will be no way for me to check on you to make sure you get somewhere safe. Keep that in mind. I can help you to disappear, but you might disappear into a trunk at the foot of someone's bed."

Sarah shivered. "Honour among thieves," she said.

Jack laughed. Honour among thieves; violence and the threat of violence; secrets held against the time they could be used to gain some advantage.

They sat in silence for a few seconds before Jack asked, "Do you have somewhere you can stay?"

"A few places."

"Are you going to be at the auction?"

"No. My job's done."

Jack's eyes wandered over her body.

"Get some different clothes," he said, "and a coat. Don't get anything that will make you stand out and don't get anything that's like what you'd normally wear. Got it?"

"OK."

"Elastic bandages."

"What?"

"Strap your breasts down. Change your silhouette." Jack laughed. "I'm working this out as I go," he said. "It's not every day I find myself in a bad novel. Do you have a hair straightener?"

"No."

"Get one. Dye your hair, straighten it. Reshape your eyebrows. Get dressed. Leave. Don't take anything with you. Go to the subway station and get some passport photographs. You've got a bit of an English accent; can you make it more pronounced without forcing it?"

"I don't know. I've never tried."

"Practice. You've got until the day after tomorrow. At six o'clock on that morning, you go to the airport. That guy Charlie, can he be trusted? If I leave something there for you, will you get it?"

"Yeah. Charlie's cool."

"OK, call to him. Tell him you're going to pick up a package at four o'clock in the morning. Don't tell him you're going to the airport. When you pick it up, tell him you'll be back later. We're cutting this pretty fine, but it's the best I can do right now.

"You pick up the package, there'll be a passport, a ticket and money in it. Tell Charlie you'll be back later, and then you go to the airport and join whatever tour group is on the ticket. All the details will be in the package. You get on the plane, and then you can decide what you want to do after that. Got it?"

Sarah's reply was soft and full of sorrow, "Got it."

"Say it back to me."

Sarah repeated what Jack had told her.

"How will I get the passport photographs to you?" she asked.

"I'm coming to that. Give me you cell."

Sarah handed over her phone.

"They're tracking you through this," Jack said, "Now they can track me for a while. We'll catch the subway, get off at different stops. I'll meet you at Oxford Circus in four hours."

"I won't be able to do all that in four hours."

"You don't have to, just get your hair done, get the photographs and get to Oxford Circus."

"OK."

"When we meet, I'll give you your phone, you give me the photographs. That's the last time we see each other. When you leave for the airport, have your phone with you, leave it on the subway, someone will steal it and that should buy you a couple of hours. Got it?"

"Got it."

"OK. Let's go."

Celeste was fast and efficient. She had absolutely no romantic feelings for Jack, but she loved him. When her daughter, Lucy, was trying to cover up her heroin addiction, it was Jack who recognised the signs. He paid for her rehabilitation. In part, this was an attempt to assuage the guilt he felt at not being able to save his father, and in part, it did. Lucy was now twenty years of age and in the top two percent of her year at university. She was studying law with her eye on the Home Office. Because of her drug experience, she wanted to take criminals off the streets.

Jack found Celeste where she always was at this time of day: in a greasy spoon at an indoor market. She sat in a corner of the café with a mug of tea and a red top newspaper. She was working on a Sudoku puzzle. Jack bought a mug of tea and a sausage roll and sat across from her. Celeste lifted the puzzle page out of the paper and passed the rest to Jack. Nothing would disturb her until she had finished.

Jack leafed through the paper. A photograph of Princess Diana covered half the front page. Underneath, a reality TV star had called a press conference to complain about media intrusion into his life. Inside the paper, Jack found the seeds of a moral crusade. Despite an alleged victory in the so-called war on terror, ninety percent of heroin in the UK comes from Afghanistan. The headline in block capitals ran: WE CAN FIND A GRAIN OF RICE FROM SPACE, BUT WE CAN'T FIND A FIELD OF POPPIES.

Beneath the headline, a picture spread over two pages, showed a masked man holding a British made rocket launcher guarding a field of poppies.

"And seven makes nine. Done." Celeste put her pencil down in triumph. She picked up her mug of tea and brought it up to her mouth, then noticed the scum that had formed on the surface. Her thick lips crinkled, and she lifted sad eyes to Jack. She put the mug to one side.

"When?" she asked.

"Tomorrow night."

Celeste let out a long breath and shook her head, looking at Jack as if he were an errant schoolboy.

"I know," he said, "but it's an emergency."

"Isn't it always? Do you have the pictures?"

"Not for another four hours."

"Four hours?"

"And I need a complete album."

Celeste started laughing. Jack leaned in towards her. "I'll give you double," he said.

"Jaaack," she drew his name out with a smile. "What have you done?"

"This isn't for me."

Celeste studied Jack for a few seconds, reading all the clues he know he offered. Slowly, Celeste's eyes lit up. "You're in love."

Jack closed up.

"Who is this girl?" she teased him.

"Can you get it done?"

"Of course I can get it done."

Jack realised his mistake and apologised. Celeste reached across the table and put her hand on his, smiling with her eyes to let him know she understood.

"What can you tell me?" This question had nothing to do with the job. Celeste would be given all the information she needed, and the less she knew, the better for all involved. But Jack was damaged in a way that endeared him to her, it had saved her daughter's life, because of that,

Celeste held out a hope for Jack that he would never entertain.

"I'm sorry, Celeste, I can't tell you anything."

"You sure?"

"Tell me about Lucy."

Jack booked Sarah on a pilgrimage to Lourdes. It always amused him that so many people look for salvation in package holidays. The people who claim that God is everywhere could not find Him without the high overhead. The only other package he could find was to Israel for a tour of the Holy Land. But given their problems with the Palestinians, and given the treatment of Israeli Bedouins, the country seemed a little busy. He was also concerned that Israel was an American satellite. Lourdes might be a tacky tourist trap, but it had the virtue of being French, and the French might be a little less willing to co-operate with what Jack considered the terrorist wing of his own government. Of course, that would not stop them from kidnapping her – French law be damned!

After making these arrangements, Jack went to his bank. He kept an English passport and twenty thousand pounds sterling in a safe-deposit box. He emptied this out, and then at various banks around the city, converted ten thousand pounds into Euros of different denominations. He bought a sewing kit so Sarah could sew the money into her clothes.

Taking the escalator down to the platform at Oxford Circus, Jack studied the faces of the blondes and brunettes coming the other way. There was no sign of Sarah. He walked along the platform, taking note of every face he could see getting off the train. Still, he did not recognise anyone. He stood back against the wall and looked at his watch. There were a few minutes to go. After two more trains had been and gone, Jack began to worry. Her time was up. If they had come for her, they would be coming for him.

"When men see a woman with a moustache, they usually don't notice the woman."

Jack turned to the woman beside him. She stood slightly stooped, wisps of silver in her slate grey hair, National Health glasses with tinted lenses. Her skin was pale and her eyebrows thick. A line of blonde and silver moustache hair along her top lip ended at a mole, from which tufts of hair stood up like spikes. She wore a brown Arran sweater, and a floral patterned skirt that reached the ground. She clutched at the strap of a satchel across her shoulder. She put a hand on Jack's arm and said again, "When men see a woman with a moustache, they usually don't notice the woman."

After dropping off Sarah's passport photographs, Jack took a tube to Heathrow and with his English passport booked a seat to his South American hideaway. It was due to leave at the same time as his flight to Boston. At best this would buy him ten or twelve hours. When he failed to show up in Boston, a phone call would send people to the penthouse.

A brown paper package, tied up with string, sat waiting for Jack at the Dorchester. He had expected an envelope with instructions for the following day. But this package was about the size of a shoebox and other than the name *Jack Higgins*, there was no writing on it, and no message had been left. The night porter said it was there when he came on duty. Masterson? Hardly. He would not want anything to distract Jack. Sarah knew better than to get in touch. The only other people Jack knew in London were Celeste and Lucy. He lifted the package, surprised by its weight. In his suite, Jack put the package on the sitting room table and stood, staring at it, considering the possibilities. Putting his money on a long shot, he telephoned Celeste in the hope that she had somehow finished Sarah's papers. Even as he dialled her number, Jack knew this was not true. In all the years he had known her, Celeste never deviated from an agreed plan. Maybe Lucy had sent him something. That explanation fell apart when he recalled their last meeting. Lucy knew what he was, and it was only for her mother's sake that she hadn't turned him in.

Jack listened to the dial tone. Celeste was in her workshop. She never answered the phone when she was working. Often she did not even hear it ring.

Jack put his ear to the box, listening for the tick-tock of a time bomb, but modern bombs do not tick. He stood up and moved away from it, crossed the room, turned and stopped. He took a half-step towards the package and stopped again. His brows knit together as he tried to understand what was happening. It may be a perfectly innocent package. If so, why was there no message? If this were a bomb, it was his first, and Jack had no idea how to deal with it. He thought about calling the police. "Hello, I'm a thief over here on business. I think someone may have sent me a bomb. Can you send someone round?"

He shook himself free from his fears and full of purpose, crossed the floor. Very carefully, he lifted the package from the table and carried it to the bathroom. He put it into the bath and plugged the drain, then turned both taps on. He stood watching the slow trickle of water. He felt a sudden need to use the toilet. He closed the toilet lid, sat down, crossed his legs and gently rocked. Blown up while taking a slash was not how he wanted to go. Somewhere in his head was the message: *bomb equals fire, water kills fire*. When the bath was full, Jack turned the taps off. He sat back on the toilet: thinking – trying to think. If the package had not blown up by the morning, he would assume it was safe and open it, unless, of course, the water had not already done that for him. Now he really did have to use the toilet.

Jack changed his clothes and went down to dinner. There were a few couples and a single woman waiting to be seated. Jack smiled at the woman; she turned away with a 'humph'. Jack opened his copy of *Lost Horizon* and rejoined Conway's party.

After dinner, Jack went to a small casino. The members were young, mainly working class; some of them there for the thrill of the game; some of them sick on the dream of easy riches: convinced that the cards would one day favour them, that every penny they lost brought them closer to wealth.

The casino put a semblance of normality back into Jack's life. He changed two thousand pounds into chips and went to the Roulette table. He watched the play for a few turns before joining in. A waitress brought him his usual Tullamore Dew.

Jack was on his second drink when he noticed a woman staring at him. Her steady gaze and the devilish play at the corners of her lips took Jack back to the train journey they had shared. He smiled at her: a bed for the night? She smiled back then turned and whispered to a woman standing beside her. The second woman's head tilted very slightly towards Jack. Her lips curled into a sly smile that may have been an invitation, but the look in her eye when she laughed said otherwise. Her hand disappeared behind the first woman, who perked up a little more. There was no invitation from either woman, but neither was there reproach. They were just enjoying themselves, they seemed to say, 'You had your fun, now we'll have ours.' Jack winked good luck to them and turned back to the game.

Jack returned alone to his hotel suite. He went into the bathroom to check on the package. Water had swollen the cardboard, but the box remained unopened. Surely if it were a bomb, something would have happened by now? Was it worth the chance? He decided to let the water melt the cardboard walls. If it were a bomb, the heavy bath would help to contain and direct the explosion upwards. There were two solid walls and the space of the sitting room between him and it. By the morning, he would have his answer.

Jack jumped awake. The room was still. He listened. A confusion of sounds from outside. He got out of bed, went to the window and pulled back the curtain. The Police had cordoned off an area at the front of the hotel, and a gathering crowd stared up at his room. The explosion in the bathroom. Then he realised there had been no explosion. Whatever held the crowd had nothing to do with him. At least the package had not been a bomb. Then what?

Jack went through to the bathroom and found a record of life floating on the water: photographs of a mother and daughter through the years. Looking back through the ages, Jack recognised the mother, but he could not place her. As she and her daughter grew older, the girl became Sarah.

Jack spread towels on the floor. One by one, he took the photographs out of the bath. He wiped them off and laid them down on the towels. He understood. To disappear so utterly was a kind of death, and if she must die then she wanted something of her to survive. He found himself looking forward to seeing her again. Perhaps in a year or two she would turn up on his doorstep. How many other women would have passed through his life by then? The question was an automatic response that Jack immediately hated.

He called down for breakfast and finally got the scrambled eggs he had ordered on his first day. When it arrived, Jack asked about the commotion outside. A campaign group had climbed onto the roof and unveiled a banner. They had somehow learned that an American television psychologist was staying at the hotel. The protesters were not concerned with meeting him, but the story would go further than if he had not been there.

After he had eaten, Jack went over the photographs with a hairdryer: cool air blowing the water away from

Sarah's face. When he finished, he packed away what could be saved and took them to his bank where they still sit in his safe-deposit box.

He arrived back at the Dorchester just in time for the car that would take him to the auction.

The journey almost exactly mirrored his first trip. There were fifty people in the auction room. Some sat waiting. Some examined the painting. Some stood talking like nervous friends, some like confident enemies. On a buffet table, bottles of champagne, caviar and toast points, delicacies arranged as art, went largely untouched. Behind the table, two servers waited for orders.

"Gentlemen," the auctioneer drew all attention to himself. "If you would like to take your seats."

All pretence of friendship evaporated now. Each man found his assigned place, picked a numbered paddle from the chair and sat down. Some fixed a Bluetooth connection to an ear.

"Welcome, Gentlemen, to the sale of the century. My name is Nicholas Parsons, and I will be your host for this evening. You all have secure connections? Yes? Good. Who will give me one hundred million dollars?"

Arms shot up like schoolboys begging for favour. Within a minute, the bid staggered among a handful of people. The painting was worthless to them, but the nation builders in their ears believed that she was priceless.

The bid stalled at five hundred million dollars. The auctioneer raised his gavel and began to count. Jack raised his paddle and the price by ten million dollars. It was his first bid. Desperate voices whispering, begging to be allowed to continue, "I can take this guy, he's a pansy!" The arguments saw some paddles raised, and others laid to rest. Jack continued to raise the bid. Soon the only other bidder was a grumpy looking man who seemed to resent every penny wasted on a second-hand painting. The bid stood at seven hundred million dollars. Masterson's instructions came back to Jack. "It will come down to you and one other person. That man is under instructions to buy the painting regardless of the expense. He will outbid you. I want you to drive the price of that thing into the billions."

At the house in Dartmoor, this had sounded fair enough, but faced with the situation, Jack began to feel nervous. However much money this other guy had behind him, there was a limit to that money, and there was a limit to his nerve. There were also limits to Jack's nerve, and those limits now came into view. He raised the bid by one hundred million dollars. His opponent topped this by another hundred million. They continued, each increasing the others bid by one hundred million dollars. Those who had dropped out now watched these two Good Old Boys go at it. Some wished their boss had the stones to stay in the fight. The bid reached one billion five hundred million dollars. It was down to Jack. Try as he might, he could not imagine anyone paying that much for a painting. He was about to lay his paddle down. Something felt wrong. On a hunch, he bid two billion dollars.

Shocked voices. Heads turned. The auctioneer stood with his gavel in the air.

"Sir? Two billion dollars?"

"Two billion dollars," Jack said.

"Two billion dollars." The auctioneer smiled. He looked over the room. "Three billion dollars, thank you Sir." The auctioneer turned to Jack. He smiled and laid his paddle down. The auction had taken less than fifteen minutes.

When the auctioneer received confirmation that the money had been transferred, he nodded to the servers. Each man stooped and stood again, holding a submachine gun. They opened fire and bodies fell. There was no drama to these deaths. The bodies simply fell. Some died before they hit the ground. The wounded and the few who escaped the bullets tried to hide among the dead while the

An Empire of Silence

gunmen stood watching. Every sound brought a burst of gunfire and silence.

Crouched behind the podium, the auctioneer watched for survivors. Some trembled in anticipation of meeting their maker, but most of these men without mercy were inwardly certain death would pass them by. One of the gunmen walked the room, and following the auctioneer's eyes, put a bullet into every head to which he was directed.

The auctioneer stood up. He looked around the room, letting out a long breath. He gestured towards the final survivor. One of the gunmen walked over to this man, "Mr. Higgins, your car is waiting."

"Jack."

Jack had just begun to enter the limo when the empty voice assaulted him. He turned his head and found the unlined face beaming from the darkness. Beside Masterson, the drinks cabinet was open, a decanter of whisky and two glasses stood ready and waiting. Jack took his seat, and the gunman closed the door.

"Tullamore Dew, isn't it?" Masterson asked. He half-filled a tumbler and offered it to Jack.

Jack slumped in his seat. Almost an innocent. He began to see how he had been used.

"Come on, Jack." As the car moved off, Masterson reached across to give Jack a drink. "You're on my team. I'm not going to kill someone who's on my team. Take the drink." It was a command.

Jack took the glass.

"Bottoms up!" Masterson raised his glass in toast. He swirled the whisky around then sipped. Jack knocked his drink back. He was thankful for the drink, he was thankful for his life, but he hated his benefactor. Masterson spread himself out more fully on his seat. He looked like a discarded Halloween costume. For several minutes, neither man said a word. Jack's thoughts were with Sarah; he wanted to get away and deliver her new passport and, from a discrete distance, see her safely onto the flight to Lourdes.

"Have you ever seen a movie called 'The Mechanic'?" Masterson asked.

"No."

"It's an old Charles Bronson movie, a very much underrated actor. It's a great movie, Jack. He plays an assassin, and for the first fifteen minutes of the movie, he does not say a word, but it is riveting. At some point, we hear an argument in the background, but it stays in the background. Charles Bronson does not say a thing, not one word.

"I was watching it last night. Do you think that movie audiences today would have the attention span for something like that? I mean in an action movie? I don't think they would. If that movie were being made today, he'd go about his business explaining to the audience why the guy deserved to die.

"He'd probably still be alive at the end of the movie. Redeemed by the love of a good woman, a puppy, or some such." Masterson laughed.

"Charles Bronson didn't live?"

"No. Do you want to know the end?"

Jack gestured for Masterson to continue.

"He had taken on an apprentice, and the apprentice was hired to kill him because he had taken on an apprentice without getting permission. The apprentice coated the inside of a wine glass with poison."

Jack was suddenly conscious of the heavy glass in his hand, the weight of it dragging on his arm. Masterson studied the progress of the question through Jack's body, and when he was satisfied that Jack honestly believed he was going to die, the old man said, "Of course, I haven't done that to you, Jack. But you should be aware, If I so choose, you will die."

For a few seconds, Jack fought the urge to give himself over to anger, but to hell with it. This ugly old fuck had been playing him for long enough. How long before Jack was no longer useful? How soon before Masterson would "so choose"? Jack would never know the time, he may never see his killer, but he would die. Right now, he had a chance.

Jack measured the distance to Masterson's neck. Two steps and a lunge. Break the glass against his head. Drag the remains down the side of his face. Bury it fatally deep in his neck. Two steps and a lunge. Jack gave himself to that instant of anger and launched himself from the seat. He collapsed on the floor.

"I said I hadn't coated your glass in poison, Jack. But don't worry, you're on my team."

Peter Hopkins – IV

Later on, everything seemed to have happened to someone else. It seemed to have happened in silence and slow motion. He could recall the crowds but not their cheers. He could see their open mouths. He could feel the voices raised in triumph. He could see the vibrations in the air carry that triumph to him. He could feel his feet leave the ground. He could feel his body rising up. For a moment, he could see nothing at all. Then he had the sensation that he was flying. Then the sky, the endless sky; the most delicate shade of blue he had ever seen. He wondered how he had never noticed it before. Then he was sitting on their shoulders, and he could see the reporters baying for a quote. He drew his gaze closer, and he could see the cheerleaders and his mind raced because he wanted to do all of them.

Looking from a private box were his mother and the man who would make his future possible. There would be a party at the weekend at this man's house, where the hometown hero would be unveiled in the manner of a new acquisition. In a few weeks, he would graduate, valedictorian of the class of nineteen seventy-three. In the fall, he would go to MIT, on a scholarship paid for by the man in the private box. After MIT, he planned to travel, to Huston and the stars.

Tonight, however, there would be Nancy. Tonight he would claim a more pressing graduation, before his teammates discovered he was still a virgin.

14/Memories Are Made of This

A strange sensation warmed Jack, a gentle rise and fall that took him back to the fairground rides of his early childhood. He dreamed himself aboard a Coney Island plastic elephant travelling through exotic imaginings to a place of safety where people listened.

He opened his eyes. He was on a cot in a small cabin. At least he was wearing his own clothes. He turned with the swell of the sea and almost fell out of the cot. A window full of stars above his head. He stood up and opened the window, breathing deeply. He looked at the sea and laughed, his days of jumping from windows were done. Dean Martin drifted down from above: *Memories Are Made of This*.

As sea air flooded the cabin, Jack began to feel a little fresher. He thought of Sarah. What had happened when she called to Charlie and found there was nothing waiting for her? Would Charlie help her? Would he recognize her with the moustache? "When men see a woman with a mustache, they usually don't notice the woman." Now sorrow. Now regret. Now there was nothing Jack could do. He thought of his own predicament.

He was somewhere on the Atlantic, with a man who held others in contempt: an arms dealer, a drug dealer, a conman of considerable flair, Masterson had planned and executed an exquisite swindle. Then Jack recalled the massacre at the end of the auction and knew he was alive only because Masterson had willed it so.

Jack knew the ship's destination; he knew there could be only one cargo; he knew that whatever part Masterson had authored for him, in the end there could be only death.

Jack tried the door; it opened into the cabin. He stepped through and walked along the corridor. He turned the corner, looking for stairs leading to the lower decks. After two more corridors, Jack found a stairway leading up. He climbed the stairs and found a door. He opened it and went out on deck. A soft mist hung in the air. Beside him rose the five stories that housed the living quarters and the bridge. There was a light coming from the bridge but no sign of activity. Even automated ships would need a crew of some description, but for the time being he was alone with the sound of the sea and the ship's engines working somewhere below him.

The door to the bridge opened, and Jack heard Dino seducing some young senorita. Someone stepped out onto the deck and closed the door. Jack recognized Clarence, the assassin who wanted to quit contract killing and get into musical theatre. He must have been in London all this time. Jack stepped back into the shadows. He waited until he heard the footsteps pass by overhead.

Five cargo holds with a crane between each one. In the third, hidden amongst the more mundane export items of Great Britain, Jack found assault rifles; pistols; revolvers; rocket launchers with cases of rockets; thousands of rounds of ammunition; fuses and timers and something he did not immediately recognize: bricks of orange putty wrapped in plastic: semtex.

Jack pieced together a thirty-minute fuse. He pushed it into a brick of semtex and replaced the lid on the box. In his mind, he saw the ship sink, and he wondered what else would happen. Would the rockets simply explode, or assault the sky and distant ships? Might bullets fired from their casing execute him?

Jack made his way to the back of the ship. He was

standing by one of the lifeboats, trying to figure out how to lower it into the sea, when he heard a voice above him.

"There you are?" Clarence stood on the gangway, at the door through which Jack had come out on deck. "Come on up. We've been looking for you."

Jack and Clarence passed through a doorway into what appeared to be a different era. The room took up most of the deck. The decor took Jack back to a brothel he had once visited in Germany.

Clarence sat in an armchair by the cabin door. Masterson's voice came from another room. "Jack, I'll be with you in a minute. Help yourself to a drink."

Jack turned towards the voice. Clarence pointed to a large globe. Jack walked over to the globe and gave it a spin. The top rolled back, revealing bottles of whisky and gin.

"The glasses are clean, Jack."

Jack looked over his shoulder. Masterson smiled from the doorway. He walked over to Jack and picked up a bottle of whisky, "You still think I want you dead?" Masterson paused. His shoulders tensed, and his knuckles turned white as he gripped the whisky bottle. "We have work to do." He concentrated on opening the bottle and pouring the whisky. He offered a drink to Jack.

"No." Jack was conscious of the passing time, the acid eating through the fuse.

Masterson nodded. He put the bottle back in its holder and closed the globe.

"So," said Masterson, "exposition. You are on my team. I do not kill people who are on my team. The people at the house, they deserved to die. We sent you to the auction to ensure the highest possible price, and I could not send one of my own people. OK?"

"Where are we going?"

"You know where we're going. You know why we're going there."

Jack didn't answer.

Masterson sat down. "Firstly, Jack, I would like to assure you, there are a number of techniques that I can and will employ if you do not give me the correct answers. Do I make myself clear?"

He had spoken so casually that Jack did not immediately grasp what he had heard.

"What's this all about?" Jack asked. A sudden pain ripped through his body, and Jack found himself on the floor. When he got his breath back, he turned to see Clarence standing over him, a pained expression on his face. Little bolts of lightning leapt between the electrodes of a stun gun in his hand.

"That was the wrong answer," Masterson said. He gestured to Clarence. Another jab from the stun gun brought Jack screaming to his knees, his eyes streaming.

"Come on, Jack," Clarence pleaded, "don't do this to me." Jack's hands shot up. His face begged for mercy. How long till the explosion?

Masterson shook his head, disappointed with Jack's obstinacy.

"In London," Masterson said, "you were seen talking quite intimately with a number of people. What did you talk about?"

Jack got up off the floor. How long till the explosion? "I'll tell you whatever you want to hear."

"Just tell me the truth. I know you were working against me."

"OK," Jack said. If Masterson were determined to uncover a conspiracy against him, Jack would do his best to help. Masterson turned to Clarence, who withdrew to his seat by the door. Jack stood shaking.

"Now, tell me who you spoke to about me."

Jack eased himself into a chair. "I didn't talk to anyone about you. You hired me to do a job. I did that job. You lied to me every step of the way, and then you drugged me."

"The woman you spoke to in the café?"

"You know about her. Sarah, what's her name?"

"No, Jack. Not her." Masterson turned to Clarence. He took an envelope from the table at his side, walked over to Jack and dropped it into his lap. Jack looked from the envelope to Masterson.

"Open it," Masterson commanded. Jack waited. Metal clicked by his ear. He turned to see the gun aimed at his head. He picked up the envelope and turned it so the mouth was facing Masterson, then ripped it open. Masterson's hands flew to his face to protect himself, he roared and Jack threw the envelope away. He looked at it, waiting for the bang. Masterson laughed.

Something caught Jack's eye. A little black book had spilled out of the envelope. Even without opening it, Jack knew what he would find. He weakened, realizing why Celeste had not answered her phone. Still shaking inside, Jack knelt down and picked up the passport. He opened it and smiled at Sarah's picture. He looked up at Masterson.

"Hate won't help you sleep at night, Jack, believe me," Masterson said.

The room shook with the end of the world. The lid of cargo hold three was blown a quarter of a mile into the air by the force of the blast. A series of explosions ripped the hull in two and sprayed bullets into the night.

Clarence flew backwards. His head cracked against the wall, leaving a sudden bloodstain like a melting poppy. As he fell to the floor, his gun went off, and a bullet passed through Jack's leg, just missing the bone. Masterson was on the floor now. He called to Jack for help.

This tangible crisis gave Jack his strength back. Being on the floor before the bomb went off had saved him from any serious knocks. On some instinct, he blocked out the pain in his leg. He searched around for Sarah's passport, found it and put it into his pocket. He picked up the gun. He struggled to his feet and went over to Masterson. Terror burned in the eyes of his once pristine face. The shining teeth now had an outline of blood. He reached out to Jack, "I think my leg's broken."

Jack looked down at Masterson's legs. His right foot twisted inwards. The ankle had snapped.

"I can't carry you. I'm sorry." Jack said. The furniture started to slide as the ship began to rise. The death rattle of metal on metal grew louder as the ship filled with water.

"I don't want to drown." It was the voice of supplication, speaking with the memory of drownings its owner had witnessed, drownings its owner had ordered, and who was now trying to regain control of a scene he had not written.

Jack hobbled to the door, his senses in revolt. The ship groaned, and the furniture moved again. He turned to look at Masterson – an abandoned baby – but Jack could do nothing to help. The ship was at thirty degrees to the water. Jack tossed the gun to Masterson and climbed through the door. Holding onto the pipes that ran along the wall, Jack pulled himself to the end of the corridor. His body fought every movement, ached to stop, to rest, to breathe, to slip into slumber, to sleep and not to dream. Facing him, a door opened onto the deck where he had tried to launch the lifeboat. He reached across the corridor and grabbed the edge of the open doorway.

The ship was rising steadily now. Jack climbed out onto the deck. The lifeboat was gone. He hobbled and stumbled over to the ship's railing and saw the lifeboat, still covered and lying low in the water. With his wounded leg, the railing was too high to climb, so Jack leaned his body across it and swung both legs over. He tried to steady himself to jump then remembered the swimming lessons of his youth. "If your shoes fill with water, they will drag you down and you will die." He hooked his right arm around the railing and attempted to kick off his shoes. One went easily, but as he tried to kick off the other shoe, Jack lost his grip on the railing and fell. He bounced against the hull once before hitting the water and sinking.

Parts of the ship fell past him, some missing him by

inches. He began to push up towards the light. He had somehow switched off the agony of the salt water washing into the bullet hole in his leg. He broke through to the air. He half swam, half flopped to the lifeboat and clung to it. He felt the current pull him towards the rapidly rising ship. If that dragged him down, he would never come up again. Concentrate. He pulled away part of the cover and found that the lifeboat was filling with water.

On the other side of the ship, the ten crewmembers were rowing happily away, knowing that while they may have to answer to an inquiry, they would not have to answer to Masterson.

15/The Captain's Guest

The sun rose, immaculate out of the darkness, streaking the sea with orange and gold. There was almost no trace of what had happened in the night, except for the body, exhausted on the upturned lifeboat.

It had taken all of Jack's strength to turn the lifeboat over and swim it to what he hoped was a safe distance. He climbed on top and watched the ship rear its backside to the sky before the ocean pulled it down. For a while, water bubbled and foamed as the ship became salvage, then there was only the sea, the stars, and colored lights blinking in the distance.

When the ship had finally disappeared beneath the water, Jack found himself marveling at the heavens. He recalled his tenth grade science teacher, Miss Breen, telling the class that when you look at the night sky, you are looking back in time, because of how long it took starlight to reach us. Miss Breen sometimes organized trips to Connecticut so the kids could look back in time. She called these trips *Expeditions to Eternity*. Although the Math teacher and some of the children's parents supervised these expeditions, stories soon began to circulate about expeditions to another eternity. There was no truth to these rumors, but parents lodged complaints, and in the absence of evidence, paranoia won the day. The trips stopped and soon after that, Miss Breen lost her job.

Sleep pulled at Jack's eyelids. The more he fought the further he fell, slipping into that luxurious confusion at the border of dreams and reality. Around him, the sea looked brilliantly blue and solid; he let his foot slip down the side of the boat to test it. The moment he broke the surface of the water, Jack's dulled nerves sharpened and pulled his leg back to the relative safety of the boat.

"Holy shit!" He looked about him, trembling, riding the lifeboat as if it were some sort of exotic fish that could return to the deep at any moment, leaving the idiot to try to straddle the ocean. Jack found himself slipping away again. He began to dream, and in his dream the world filled up with grey. He looked up, his eyes widening. His tense muscles relaxed, and a broad smile spread across his face. He laughed. The colored lights that had winked at him in the darkness had grown to become a destroyer.

During the night, the destroyer had taken on a passenger. He arrived by helicopter from an aircraft carrier on its way to the Persian Gulf. He handed the Captain a new set of orders. They were to keep out of range of the cargo ship, to follow and observe. An hour and a half after the explosion aboard that ship, the destroyer picked up her crew. Their assurance that they were the only survivors was relayed down to the Captain's guest. He turned his computer to the Captain and pointed to a number on the screen.

"That's what we're after." "That," was Jack.

After they had picked him up, Jack was taken to the infirmary. His bullet wound was dressed, and tests carried out. The Chief Medical Officer reported to the Captain's quarters.

"His heart is a little sluggish, more than it should be for a man of his age, but, all things considered, he's doing well."

The visitor turned and looked at the papers on the desk beside him. He laid his hand on top of them and tapped his finger a few times, then turned back to the Chief Medical Officer. "I'm going to need all of your data, as well as any samples you've collected from him."

"I'll get it ready." The Chief Medical Officer turned to leave.

"Doctor."

He turned. The other man slid a file from a bundle on the desk. He opened it.

"Do you know why his heart is sluggish, Doctor?" He pushed the file away and selected another. This was the file he wanted. He looked up at the Doctor. The Doctor paused. The truthful answer was not necessarily the right answer, and he had built a career on knowing when to be truthful and when to be right. In situations like this, the questioner's voice usually gave some instruction either way. With this man, however, the Doctor could find no clue as to what was required.

"I can't give you a diagnosis, if that's what you're looking for." The Doctor tried to pitch his voice to say he knew why Jack's heart was sluggish, and that he could be trusted to keep the secret. The visitor gave the appearance of considering this new information.

"Is that everything?" The Doctor's eyes were stinging. He was eager to get away. The visitor reached down the far side of the desk and withdrew a small brown bottle from his case. He put the bottle on the desk in front of the Doctor.

"Give him a shot of this when he wakes up."

The Doctor picked the bottle up and turned it in his hand. There was no label; there were no marks of any kind to indicate what the bottle contained.

"What is this?" The question was not an act of defiance; it was a request for information.

"It's an order."

The Doctor surprised himself by putting the bottle back down on the desk. "I am the Chief Medical Officer onboard this ship."

The Captain's guest considered this and smiling, nodded his head. "Thank you, Doctor."

Within the hour, the ship received a message calling the Doctor to Washington. He left that night. Shortly afterwards, one of the ship's medics, a newly minted Navy Doctor with one eye on a Government job, was interviewed privately in the Captain's quarters. When Jack woke up, the eager young medic administered the shot.

The surge of energy Jack felt made him realize how drained he had been since – when? The smell of hot food brought him back to the ship. He sat up in bed eating and taking in his surroundings.

"When you finish that we have some questions for you." Jack took no comfort from the medic's American uniform.

The man in grey opened a file, carefully removed a paperclip from the top left-hand corner and spread the pages before him. Although he had already studied this file and could recite its contents from memory, habit and good practice made him scan each page again. When he came to a salient fact, his finger stopped moving, he made a short 'Hm' sound.

When he finished, he gathered the pages together, replaced the paperclip with the same deliberation with which he had removed it, then put the pages back into the folder, and closed the file. He turned to Jack.

"How..." Jack asked.

"I'll answer your questions later," the man in grey cut in. He recited Jack's academic record, his triumphs in the classroom and on the football field. However, he noted that Jack had not belonged to any clubs. He rattled off key points from Jack's social security record. After a brief account of Jack's father's two tours of duty in Vietnam, the man in grey seemed genuinely sad to sum up the old soldier's life with silence. This was not a mark of respect.

"Get to the point," Jack said.

"The point," the man in grey paused for dramatic effect, "the point is: this is just to let you know."

The words dragged Jack back to his bedroom in the dark, waking up to find the girl gone and the silhouette in the chair. "This is just to let you know." That silhouette turned out to be Clarence, a different kind of criminal to this one, but for both, their stock in trade appeared to be murder. The man in grey took an A4 envelope from his briefcase and spilled its contents onto the desk.

"I have no quarrel with you about any of these people. These people have no call to take up space in this world."

They were photographs of crime scenes. He picked one up. "Recognize him?"

Despair closed Jack's eyes. Sickness swam in his stomach, and his head turned away. There was almost nothing to recognize in the photograph. Part of the head was missing and long silver hair, pasted by blood to the skin, obscured what was left. The man in grey put the photograph down and picked up another: a photograph of a photograph. Smiling from a silver frame, Jack saw the Texan who had been handing out candles at the war protest. A strawberry blonde stood beside him with a broad smile on her face. It was their wedding day.

"We know you met with this person."

"I didn't meet with him. I met him. There's a difference."

"What did you talk about?"

"Don't you know what we talked about?"

The man in grey tried a different photograph. This one showed the remains of a woman. Jack recognized the pink hair and the ladybug pattern on her oversized sweater: the righteous hippy chick whose brother had been killed in Iraq.

"We know you don't believe in burning the flag."

"I don't believe in the so-called war on terror either." Jack's voice was cold. If he was being accused of murder, why the preamble?

"It's fairly common knowledge, Jack, there is no war on terror, never was. What's called the war on terror is just a distraction. This is the real war." He threw down another photograph, another, another, another: all of them scenes of atrocity; the people butchered beyond recognition.

"The only thing to connect all of these people is you."

Jack hardly heard; he was still looking with horror at the photographs. The twisted remains in one drew fragments from his memory and, putting them together, Jack learned why Tony had not been at the rendezvous. Broken body parts in another picture assembled themselves into the face of Celeste.

"Oh Jesus." Emotion shook Jack's body, tried to escape, but he was a well-practiced jailer and contained the threat. At some point in the future, he knew he would break down, but not now, not in front of this bastard. Holding onto the picture of Celeste, Jack let the others fall. His finger raised itself, as if to make a point, but fell back into frustrated silence. The finger moved again, stabbing the air, and again the finger fell. Finally, in surrender, Jack got his words out.

"She has a daughter."

"That's enough for now."

Jack was taken to the brig. He tried to strike up a conversation with his guard, but the sailor was under strict orders not to communicate with the prisoner in any way, shape or form. He sometimes wondered about the sanity of his leaders.

Her voice drifted down. Jack rolled over and looked up into those dark eyes that he loved. He filled himself up with her features. He reached up and touched the face of the woman he loved and had killed. She spoke again. He shuddered and pulled away, banging his head against the wall. This was no dream. She was there, towering above the cot. Her hands flew out to calm him down. "Jack."

No. She was the wrong woman. He sat up and looked

at her, trying to connect her with this new nightmare. She spoke.

"How are you feeling?"

"Sarah?"

Sarah hesitated, uncertain whether to ask her question. "I've arranged for you to be released," she said, "once we get home you'll be a free man."

"And what about you?"

Sarah thought she could detect bitterness in his voice; was it his bitterness or if she had put it there to make her life easier?

"We need to know something first."

Jack withdrew a little into himself. He turned his empty gaze on Sarah and a chill of murder ran through her. It was a horror she had never felt and in that horror she could imagine Jack killing those people. For the first time since meeting him, Sarah had the feeling that Jack did not exist in the same way as people: as a distinct personality. What she found in the brig was wreckage; a man cobbled together from snapshots and stories of untouchable people. He had an air of loss that is almost never spoken of, and on those occasions that it is mentioned, it is passed off lightly.

"I need to know something?" he asked.

"What is it?"

"You know what it is?" Jack waited for Sarah to respond, even to lie, but she said nothing.

"What am I doing here?" Jack asked.

Sarah considered her answer. She began to speak, and then stopped herself. She dismissed the guard. "OK," she said, "I'll tell you what I know." She paused for Jack to respond. When he didn't, she looked at the floor; at the window. She ran her tongue along the backs of her teeth.

"Have you heard of technetium-99m?" she asked.

Jack waited.

"It's a radioisotope used in nuclear medicine," Sarah said. "It's got a half-life of six hours."

"Which means?"

"I'm not sure exactly. The thing is, it's harmless." As she spoke, Sarah watched to see if Jack was putting things together. She did not want to be the one to tell him this.

"You remember when you found me?"

The image of Sarah sprawled out in the bath filled Jack's mind. He softened a little. "And this stuff was injected into us?"

"Yes."

"So we're radioactive?"

"No, it's perfectly safe."

"Perfectly safe?"

"I don't know. I suppose so. But what we were injected with was a modified version."

"So, what? We're an experiment?"

Sarah had no answer. Her eyes followed Jack around the room as his mind chased another betrayal.

"You know, there are some people, out there, who think that the federal government is a conspiracy."

Sarah reached for Jack's hand. "I don't understand?"

He brushed her off. "Why?"

"What?"

"Why?"

"They wanted Masterson. Before you, they didn't even know his name."

Jack stopped. He wondered how wise it would be to tell her that Masterson was dead. "What's he got to do with it?"

"They've been after him for years, I told you about Prague. You were the first real lead. They injected you thinking they could trace you back to him."

He sat, silent and contemptuous, waiting for her to continue.

"I don't know," she said. "They don't know what safeguards Masterson has."

Jack thought about this, and then asked, "Why did they inject you?"

"Because I was there."

Jack waited, lost. "How do you know this thing is safe? How do you know we're not going to waste away? How do you know we're not going to be dead this time next week?"

"I have to know." Her hand reached for his. Again, he pulled away. They sat searching each other's face for – something. They seemed to come to an arrangement.

"He's dead," Jack spoke to the floor. They sat in silence for several minutes. Then the room filled with the sound of the door opening. The man in grey stepped into the brig.

"You can go now," he said to Sarah. Tragedy seared the face she turned on Jack. She tried to communicate to him that she too was a prisoner, but he had already moved on, trying to prepare for his next interrogation.

16/Home

JACK

Jack entered his apartment and closed the door. He felt instantly lighter. Once again, the sun's rays reaching out from the painting touched him and lifted him. He opened the living-room door, and a moment later found himself laughing. When he was last here, there was a mess of milk and cereal spilled across the floor. The couch was overturned, and the broken pieces of a breakfast bowl were scattered near the door. The room he entered now was spotless. Had Masterson sent someone to clean up? Jack poured a glass of Tullamore Dew and sat down.

Breathing in the aroma of the whisky, Jack considered turning himself in; of confessing to his life as a thief. That might make him worthless for whatever they had planned. A confession would also make him a jailbird, whose cage would undoubtedly open whenever they wanted. Would a confession get him killed?

Before going home, Jack had taken a blood test. While awaiting the results, he re-established his old routine, the park, bookshops, brothels and bars. Every day, he went running, setting out and returning home before the morning rush hour. He reread *Fever Dream* by George RR Martin, racing through the story of vampires on a Mississippi steamboat. Then the day came when Jack had to phone for the results of his blood test.

He made the call. Each stuttering ring of the phone

tempted Jack to answer the question himself. There was no relief in the sound of the receiver at the other end being picked up.

"Could I speak to Doctor Eisler, please?"

"Jack, can you come in?"

"What's up?"

"It's fine, it's fine. I just need to have a word with you. Can you come in?"

"Of course." Jack hung up the phone.

The receptionist scrolled through the day's appointments.

"There's no Jack Higgins listed. Are you sure you made an appointment?"

"No. The Doctor called me and asked me to come in."

The receptionist let out a heavy breath. "Have a seat and I'll go check." She turned away. These special patients were a damn nuisance. Jack looked in at the waiting room. It was filled with cuts and bruises, coughs and cranks.

"Jack."

Doctor Eisler stood by the door to his office. He waved Jack over. They went in and wasted a minute in chitchat.

"Have a seat," the Doctor said. He sat opposite and pulled his chair a little closer.

"I've got good news and I've got bad news."

Jack gestured for the Doctor to begin. He leaned forward in his chair and clasped his hands together. "Good news first." He opened his hands as if making an offering. "You're clean."

Jack breathed deeply and nodded his head, smiling at the Doctor. "And the bad news?"

"The bad news is that someone else has got a copy of these results."

"Yeah. I thought that might happen. But how do you know?"

"I have someone at the lab that I keep paid to assure

privacy for my patients."

Jack went home. He now knew his next move; it had been decided for him by the man in grey.

Under the floorboards, sealed in plastic, were the details of the life Jack had created, but hoped to never use. If he were going to be free, he could no longer exist. Everything that tied Jack to his life had become worthless. He was surprised at how easily he could turn his back on everything, especially the money, the millions of dollars in South America. One day some government man would collect the money, or some lowly bank employee, banished to dormant accounts, would notice what had happened and retire.

Jack removed one of the floorboards and felt around for the airtight container. Inside was an Irish passport, a bunch of keys and his wedding ring. He slipped the ring onto his finger. It felt alien after so many years. He thought about Celeste's daughter, Lucy. He wanted to do something for her, to ease her passage through life. He had nothing but the proceeds of crime, and that would make her a target; the only thing he could offer her was the prospect of murder or jail. The thought left him feeling impotent. He let it go. Celeste had been as much a friend as Jack allowed himself, but she was dead – end of story. No doubt, he would read about Lucy in the papers from time to time. If she really did go to the Home Office, Lucy would be putting people like Jack in jail. She may already be after him.

Jack looked through the passport and laughed a little to himself. In school, he had gotten into a fight when someone called, "Hey, Irish." He was an American, born and raised in New York City. His father had been born and raised in New York City. He was American – not Irish – not Irish-American – American. Now he was preparing to go on the run disguised as a Mick. He recalled the irony of finding out that the writer Jack Higgins, from whom he had taken his name, came from Belfast.

There were four years left on the passport. He would need to have a few stamps added, including one for Montenegro, his ultimate destination. The keys were for safe deposit boxes in Europe where Jack kept ready cash. He thought about writing the Great American Novel. He could find someone to front the project, some failed writer or actor. He brushed aside this nonsense and focused on the problem at hand.

It was three days later when Jack got a call from the doorman of his building; the old man made no attempt to hide the surprise in his voice. Jack had a visitor.

SARAH

Sarah's New York was not the Park Avenue world to which she had been born; neither was it the New York of tourist brochures; although she took both of those as starting points in searching for her own perfect New York City. She told herself she was searching for the New York made familiar by Lou Reed and John Rechy. Sarah did not know it, but her version of an authentic city had more to do with sitcoms than the savagery of loneliness. She spent her first legal Christmas prowling bars, looking for the perfect New York crowd and the perfect New York jukebox. She found her perfect New York apartment, a loft in Brooklyn: fifteen hundred square feet of freedom.

Sarah signed a year's lease and moved in. She immersed herself in this world until one night when her pick-up told her that fucking her was like throwing a sausage down Park Avenue. When they first met each other, four hours earlier, and he heard the money in her voice, he decided to fuck the bitch to within an inch of her life. While they were having sex, he found himself captivated by the sight of his thumb on her throat; he wondered how many pounds of pressure it would take to end her. He laughed, but part of him felt that to come this far and not strangle her would be a crime.

Sarah never knew how close she came to death, but something about her ideal New York felt wrong. When her lover fell asleep, she left the apartment. She took a cab to the Hilton and spent the night there. The following morning she paid off the lease on her apartment and started again. She found a loft near NYU and enrolled in an art course. She began an affair with one of her lecturers. The affair ended when Sarah entered her sophomore year. She discovered she had a talent for the mechanics of painting, but after months of trying, she decided that she did not have the first clue as to how she might create an original work.

Sarah left the course. She spent her days amusing herself by making copies of the fashionable dead: Picasso, Braque, Matisse, Schell, Klimt, Monet, Manet, Davis and Warhol, all passed through her imagination without touching her and without her exerting any influence on the work. She never tried to pass these paintings off as the real thing.

A friend was throwing an end of the world party. His play had closed after its first night on Broadway. He was so deeply in debt that he had no reason to worry about ever paying it off. Somebody would rescue him. Until then, there was nothing to do but throw a party. Sarah had been there for half an hour and was getting ready to leave, when her host took her by the arm and led her through the apartment, searching for someone he described as *a delightful freak.*

The delightful freak had been invited as a showpiece. He was overweight with dyed hair and too smooth skin. He held his champagne flute with exaggerated delicacy. His thumb and forefinger pinching the stem, his other fingers fanned out. There was something mocking about his whole appearance. He complemented Sarah on her work. He offered her ten thousand dollars for a copy of Georges Braque's *The Weeding Machine*. Sarah turned the money down but offered to do the painting anyway.

"Now who turns down ten thousand dollars?" He asked the question playfully, as if the answer meant nothing to him.

"Trust-Fund Kids," Sarah said. She seemed to resent being a trust-fund kid, yet she was happy enough to live off it.

The delightful freak looked a little closer, seemed to recognize someone, asked her a few questions, and then he told her who she was.

"In that case," she said, "I'll take your money." She used the money to move to London where she continued her new life of adventure. She moved onto documents, passports and wills. One Honorable man has her to thank for his position. Two years later, the Special Branch arrested her under the prevention of terrorism act. Shortly after the American authorities were contacted, Sarah was 'disappeared' by the man in grey.

That was then ...

This is now: after her debriefing, Sarah caught the first available flight to London, and the comfort of her flat at Notting Hill. When she opened her front door, she found a note from the post office and an A4 envelope waiting for her. She dropped them onto a small side table next to the couch, and took a hot shower, then curled up in bed and tried to sleep. She was exhausted, she spent half an hour tossing and turning but sleep eluded her. She was thinking about Masterson; she did not want to think about him: she had spent the last few years trying to track him down.

Nine years earlier, the man who killed everyone who might be able to identify him had let her live. They had not met since the night in New York when he made his proposition, still, he had everyone at the auction killed because they had encountered Jack.

Sarah got out of bed. She put on a pair of cotton pants and a tee shirt and went through to the living room. She turned the television on and caught the beginning of *I Walked with a Zombie*. While the credits rolled, she went to the kitchen and got a beer. As she sat back on the couch, Sarah noticed the post. It would keep until morning.

From somewhere Sarah heard a voice. Someone was telling her to wake up. She looked at the television, wondering why it was talking to her. Then she realized she had been asleep.

She stretched, yawned, and turned the television off. She noticed the post, picked up the envelope and opened it. Inside was a sheaf of pages; the writing was double-spaced and began,

Dear Sarah, I hope you enjoy the painting.

As Sarah read, sorrow engulfed her, but it was not until she had collected the package, brought it home and opened it that she broke down. Sitting before the painting Masterson had commissioned almost a decade earlier, Sarah wept until she was weak. She wept for his beauty corrupted by greed. She wept for the hundreds now dead on the word of the monster he became. She fell with her tears down to anger and laughed. She never found out why.

17/Into This Domestic Setting

The sparkle of the chandelier rhymed with the sparkle of the silverware, as Jessica Whitely picked a fork from the table, and held it to the light to inspect the preparations for the ball which was due to begin seven hours later. Holding the fork before her, Jessica's eyes refocused and her heart swelled as, between the tines, she saw her love framed in the doorway.

"Alice."

"I stopped being Alice a long time ago." Sarah's unforgiving eyes withered the hope that had briefly blossomed in her mother's breast.

"I'm sorry. Sarah." Jessica put the fork down. Practice kept the smile on her face and her emotions in check. She began the journey across the dining room. Sarah waited where she was, despite the life she had lived since leaving home, the thought of entering the dining room without permission still made her flinch. The scars on her back began to itch. She could feel the darkness of the room where, as a child, she had been disciplined.

"What's the party for?" Sarah asked. Jessica turned to face the room. "Oh, your father. Would you like some coffee?"

"Yes, please. Thank you."

Jessica led the way to her private sitting room. As much as she wanted to hug her daughter, she was afraid of how it would be received. Their relationship had always been strained, and Jessica could sense that the woman who walked with her now was no longer hers. She opened the double doors to her private sitting room and entered. For Sarah, this room had once been a place of safety; she could feel those sensations rising in her again. She pushed them down.

Jessica rang for coffee. Sarah looked around, matching the room to her memories. The furniture, when it was new, was the height of modernism, now, it was retro chic. To her left was the roll top desk with the secret compartment she was not supposed to know about. The carpet looked ratty, like it had seen a few years traffic, but it was probably the most expensive carpet in New York. Jessica had it especially woven and aged until it was exactly what she wanted. The wallpaper, also handmade, was re-hung every year. In the centre of the wall on Sarah's right; her parent's wedding portrait, or, to be precise, half a portrait. The original spread over two canvases, one for each person. The groom, in shallow dimensions, almost flat, was painted in cheap acrylic, giving him a plastic look and feel. Behind him, a blasted landscape and crumbling pillars, in shades of purple, with clouds of muted grey and blue. The background carried over to the portrait of Jessica, but she had more dimension than her husband. Her tragic smile and alert eyes broke through the canvas, but a finger pressing against the picture plane dispelled any hope of escape. They were extraordinary paintings, much more so than the scope of these words. As a girl, Sarah spent hours at a time lost in them, without knowing why. Both canvases were contained within a gaudy gold frame. Now, only her mother smiled from the wall. She was still within the original frame, but now she was married to the weeping willow wallpaper.

"What happened?"

Jessica turned. "What?" Her eyes jumped from Sarah to the canvas. "Oh, that's been like that for years. I don't know."

Something about the old woman made Sarah feel like

an intruder. Despite herself, she began to feel sorry for her mother.

"You should come to London."

"I was in London. Last year. Remember?"

Sarah pushed the barb aside. "Come and stay."

"Now Sarah."

They were interrupted by a knock at the door. "Come in."

The door opened and a man, about fifty, wheeled in a trolley loaded with coffee, fine china and whole-wheat scones. Deep lines divided his face into sections, making him look like he had been put together from a kit. He smiled at Sarah. Fear dragged her back to her twelve-year-old bed and the man who woke her up one night by forcing his way into her body. She had tried to scream, but his hand was clamped so tightly over her mouth she could hardly breathe. She bit him as best she could, and saw pleasure in his eyes. He came to her again the next night, and every night until the girl moved away. Through the years of rape, Alice had tried to tell her parents, but her father was busy running his empire, and her mother was busy running hers: a charity that rescued children from abusive families.

"You remember my daughter?" Jessica smiled as she introduced them. "Sarah, you remember Maurice?"

Did she know? Did Mom know more than she let on?

"Welcome home," Maurice said.

"Thank you, Maurice," Jessica said. She stepped out onto the balcony and looked down on Central Park. Maurice winked at Sarah as he left the room. Sarah fought off the instinct to turn away. She put all the rage and hate she had into her eyes and looked at Maurice. Now, for the first time, she saw fear. Jessica returned, lighter, and sat on the couch. "So, what have you come to see me about?"

Now she was faced with it, Sarah almost did not want to continue. She settled herself across from her mother, picked up the coffee pot and began to pour; as if this action were a salve to soothe the sting. By putting her questions into this domestic setting, she hoped to ... what? She had never felt this naked, and her only knowledge of these situations came from movies.

"I came to ask you about dad."

"Well, of course, you know that your father loves you." Jessica took the offered cup.

"I'm not talking about your husband."

Neither woman heard the cup hit the floor. Jessica regained her composure enough to wave Sarah away.

"I want you out of here." Jessica struggled to keep her voice calm.

"Mom?"

"Sarah. Leave."

"First, I want you to tell me about Peter Hopkins."

At the sound of his name, Jessica stopped shaking. Her brows knitted together as she searched her memories but found no reference to anyone called Peter Hopkins.

Sarah sat back down. "It's OK, mom."

Jessica was lost. "What's OK?"

Sarah reached across and took her mother's hand, stroking the back with her thumb, an action she recalled from childhood, when Jessica did the same thing for her to comfort her in secret: the mother passing some of her strength to the daughter.

"Sarah, I don't know any Peter Hopkins."

"He was given the first scholarship."

While Jessica tried to recall the name, Sarah attempted to deal with her own confusion. Masterson may have lied, but there was definitely something going on with her mother.

"Yes. He was the star quarterback at the high school," Jessica said.

"Tell me about him."

Jessica told Sarah almost exactly the same story that Masterson had sent her.

"Did you sleep with him?" Sarah asked. She needed to

hear her mother deny the allegation.

"What's this about?"

"You know what it's about."

The pause before Jessica answered left Sarah wondering if she could trust what her mother was going to tell her. "No."

"Is he my father?"

Jessica looked past her daughter to the wedding painting, and in her memory returned to the early nineteen seventies, to Elvis in New York.

She was sitting in the front row of the balcony, loving the show. She saw some orange-haired kook walk up the central aisle. At the top of the aisle, he turned and took his front row seat. Jessica resented the intrusion: just because the guy's got money thinks he can turn up late for the King. On stage, the King, who must have noticed, played on.

A few rows behind Jessica sat a man with no interest in Rock 'n' Roll. He was the same age as Elvis and had grown up listening to Frank Sinatra and his Rat Pack, (His father told him the real Rat Pack was Humphrey Bogart and his crowd). He had been sketching Elvis when he noticed the flash of orange and from there he found the girl. He amended his sketch to include the two of them, turning the colour into a conduit between the King and his court. The artist wanted to say something to the girl, but he did not know how.

Two months later, Jessica graduated from college with a degree in English Literature, and went out to celebrate. Some of her friends took her to an art exhibition. They had someone they wanted her to meet. Jessica did not care about art or artists, but after four years of frat boys who thought dead poets would get them into her bed, she was ready for people who had skipped college and gone into the world.

Standing before the painting, Jessica recalled the

concert and the intruder, but she did not recognize that she was the profile in shadow. She turned back to her friends, eager to meet the man they had promised her.

Sin-D came clattering over, with high heels, immaculately shaved chest and perfect make-up, she turned more heads than some of those who had been born women.

"Jessica. Jessica. Come with me." Sin-D took Jessica by the elbow and began to lead her across the room. "Andy's here."

"Andy?"

"Yes, sweetheart."

The penny dropped when Jessica saw the crowd gathered around a fey looking figure dressed in black. Before Sin-D had a chance to effect the introduction, one of Jessica's uptown friends waylaid them. Controlling her excitement, the friend looked doubtfully at Sin-D and turned to Jessica, "He's here!"

"Antonia, I don't –"

"Do not say that. I have been trying to land him for the past year, and it hasn't worked. So, if I can't have him, he's going to someone that I love. That's all there is to it."

"Excuse me," Sin-D cut in, "but we have a prior engagement."

Antonia turned on her. "Can I see your invitation?"

"Antonia, this is my cousin, Sin-D. Sin-D, Antonia."

"Well, Cindy, I am about to introduce my friend to the man she is going to marry. I'm sure whatever you've got planned can't possibly be as important as that."

While they argued, Jessica slipped away. She had spotted someone standing before the painting of Elvis. He was the only person in the room paying any attention to the work. She went over and stood beside him. She was about to speak when he turned to her. He smiled. "What do you think?" He nodded towards the painting.

"I don't know anything about art."

"Well, do you like it?"

"I was at that concert."

"But do you like the painting?"

"Yeah. Is it yours?"

"No. It's yours."

"What!"

"If you don't like it, pick out whatever you want."

"What about your exhibition?"

"Oh, I'm not the artist."

"You're not?"

"I just bought out the exhibition. So, pick whatever painting you like, and I'll have it delivered to you when the show closes."

"Who are you?"

"I'm sorry," he held out his hand, "George Whitely." They shook hands. That was the last time the Whitely name mean nothing to Jessica.

He introduced her to the artist, a soft-spoken man who sparkled in her presence.

Within the year, Jessica and Whitely were married. Before that, her soon to be father-in-law brought her to meet the man who was to paint the wedding portrait.

The painter had changed, he seemed more confident, but something about his demeanor told Jessica that he was playing a role. They sat drinking coffee while the old man explained how a portrait should be painted. He named a few artists whose work he had seen in Germany during the nineteen-thirties. The Painter made some remarks about degenerates. The old man misunderstood and berated Warhol and *other Jews*. Nobody corrected him.

The following week Jessica returned alone to the studio. She could feel the painter shaking inside as he set to work. As much as he wanted her, he wanted her gone.

"You know, I can do this from a photograph. You don't need to be here."

"I don't want it done from a photograph. I want you to paint me."

He stopped what he was doing and looked at her

properly for the first time; something about her was far too old.

"I thought George sent you over."

"No. He wanted Warhol to do them. He said a couple of Warhol's would be worth more."

"That's not why he wanted Warhol to do them. He's right, though, a couple of Warhol's would be worth a lot more."

"No."

"Do you love him?"

"Of course I love him," Jessica said. A moment and she added, "Why do you never clean your windows?"

"What's out there?"

Jessica went to the window. She wiped the condensation away and peered through the glass and the grime on the other side.

"Manhattan," she said.

At their next meeting, they had sex, and he became her "three o'clock, Thursday afternoon." The painting progressed more slowly now, Whitely from a photograph, Jessica from life. The affair ended when Jessica became pregnant. Uncertain of how George felt about children, and afraid to jeopardize her position, she dropped subtle hints about having a baby. His lack of enthusiasm stopped her from making any announcement just yet, she would work on him.

Peter Hopkins – V

George Whitely relaxed into a deeply cushioned chair. He took a fistful of popcorn from a bucket at his side; he tossed some into his mouth and then took a long pull at the straw that reached up from a 32oz soda.

He stifled a belch and for a moment seemed embarrassed that such a vulgar sound should come from him. He pressed a button on a remote control and the screen in front of him flickered to life. The woman on the screen looked like Elizabeth Taylor, there was no sound, but he could see she was talking to someone who was in shadow.

As George watched the woman undress, the shape of her body filled him with a sense of wonder. The woman walked naked to the shadows and, reaching out, took the hand of the person who was sitting there. She pulled him to her, and George could see he was the young football hero and aspiring poet: what was his name? The woman pulled the boy to her and drawing his hand along her body, pushed his fingers inside of her. His face flushed. The woman kissed him, and as she did so, she unbuttoned his jeans and moved her hands to his hips. Lowering herself to her knees, she pulled his jeans to his ankles and took the boy in her mouth.

As he watched the sex scene unfold, George continued to eat his popcorn, drink his soda. He laughed as he watched the woman take the condom from the boy and throw it on the fire. She led him over to the bed, kissed him and whispered in his ear, then bent over the footboard of the bed and spread her legs.

The boy looked confused. He mumbled something as he approached the woman. She turned to him, her eyes full of surprise, her face full of joy as she laughed and shook her head. She reached between her legs, guided his penis into her and pushed back.

As he watched the rapid, awkward sex on screen, George took a moment to make a note: Get sound!

Almost as soon as they had begun, they were finished, and in his cinema, George tried to look between the woman's legs to see if there was anything there.

The boy moved away from the woman, his head turning awkwardly, his eyes cast down. He mumbled. The woman turned to him with a generous smile and spoke. She ruffled his hair and left the room.

George Whitely turned the screen off. He was satisfied. He knew he had married the right woman. He pushed a button in his armrest and ordered his projectionist to start the movie.

18/The John Wayne Ideal

Jack opened the door to Sarah and once again he was struck by her presence. Obeying a long suppressed instinct, he pulled her to him to kiss her. She turned her head. Jack stepped away, and they stood looking at each other, not sure what to do next. Jack closed the door. He held out his hand towards the living room.

Sarah's eyes leapt from box to box. She turned to Jack, searching for some assurance that this was a put-on.

"You're leaving?"

"Those people you work for –"

"I don't work for them," she cut in, her words almost running together.

Jack's lips curled into a smile that Sarah had seen too often.

"Believe what you want," she said. "I don't work for them. I don't work for anyone. Masterson is dead. They only wanted me to get to him, and then you came along; they decided you were a better bet."

"Do you want a drink?"

Sarah did not answer.

"There's a bottle of whisky in that box." Jack pointed to a stack of boxes by the couch. He left the room. Sarah went to the couch and sat down, she opened the first box. It was filled with photographs. She thought about her pictures. What had become of them? As she replaced the lid, something caught her eye.

"Not that one."

Sarah turned, afraid she had been caught.

Jack stood at the door with two glass tumblers. "Next one over." He nodded. He crossed to a chair and sat facing Sarah. He put the glasses down on the table. Sarah found the bottle of Tullamore Dew; it was half-empty, and she wondered had anyone helped him with it. She opened the bottle and poured two glasses.

"You did that like a pro," Jack said with a smile. He picked up his drink. "This is the finest whisky in the world."

"My dad preferred his own."

"He makes his own whisky?"

"In Kentucky."

Jack took a sip from his glass. He held the whisky in his mouth for a moment, almost chewing it, before letting the warm liquid run down his throat. "So, what do you want?"

Sarah put her glass down. She told Jack everything about Masterson, about the painter, about Whitely, about her mother. Shadows lengthened as her story unfolded, deepening the darkness of her life and creating an intimacy she had not intended. Jack felt himself dissolve in the whisky and the evening and the rhythm of her words. He found that her eyes were too much; they had an openness that left him lightheaded. He recalled a trick from years ago; he stared at the bridge of her nose and let her look into his eyes. He found his attention drawn down to her mouth. Her words disappeared in the sound of her voice. That sound, and her parting lips, held him in thrall. She finished her story in darkness and found him beside her. Neither one could say when he had crossed the floor. He kissed her and pulled away. The taste of her was all wrong. It took a moment to register with him that this was a different woman. He almost did not want to go on, but surrendered instead to memory and wrapped her body in his.

As Jack and Sarah made love, their coupled bodies crushing each other in sheets of sweat, he whispered his undying love.

Sarah stiffened. "Who's Elisabeth?"

Jack's erection withered inside her. He rolled off and lay on his back staring at the ceiling. Sarah propped herself up on the bed and turned to him, searching his face for an answer.

"She's my wife," he said, without a trace of emotion. "She's dead."

The matter of fact way in which he reported his wife's death pained Sarah. Her instinct was to offer some sort of comfort, but the distance she now felt between them disallowed that possibility. After a few moments, she asked, "Is Elisabeth – "

Murder flashed in Jack's eyes. Sarah could feel it in his voice when he spoke. "The subject is closed." He got out of bed and left the room. A few moments later, he came back with Sarah's clothes and threw them onto the bed. "You have to leave." He stood, silhouetted in the doorway. Sarah sat up, watching him.

"You have to leave, now," he said.

Reluctantly, Sarah got out of bed and began to dress. Jack went back to the living room. Frustrated anger ached for expression but would have to wait until she was gone. Never let people see you weak, or they will grind you down to dust, especially if they talk about how men should be sensitive and not afraid to cry. Experience had shown Jack that when a woman sees any kind of weakness in a man she will forever regard him as something less than a man. Despite all prostrations to the contrary, the *John Wayne Ideal* still held: a man must be able to cry, but he must not actually do it.

Three years after his wife's death, a woman saw Jack cry. She had been trying to fix him up with one of her girlfriends, when a chance remark touched something in Jack, and he started to bawl. Up until that point, Jack had not shed a tear for his wife, and the friend had frequently criticized him for being unfeeling. Now she suggested that maybe what he really needs are male friends "Perhaps in the style of the ancient Greeks." She laughed.

"You fucking bitch." Jack threw her out.

At the sound of Sarah's approach, Jack retreated into a corner. He watched her come into the room and stop. She stood in a sliver of morning; sunlight made a halo of her hair, her face was scarred with concern. The sting of cowardice brought Jack out of hiding. He felt foolish, realizing there was nothing to fear from this woman.

"We were going on our honeymoon," he said. "We had a breakdown. I went to have a look at the engine, I didn't even know anything about cars, but ... I told her to put up the triangle, the, hazard, thing ... she was hit by a car.

"Some kid ... his first car ... racing ... slammed straight into her. Then later I found out she was pregnant. She wasn't that far gone. She hadn't said anything to me. I don't even know if she knew.

"The kid who crashed into her, he ... he got off the hook. Because that's what happens when you've got money."

Not knowing what to say, Sarah took Jack's hand and held it, caressing the back with her thumb. She kissed him.

"Hey, shit happens," he said.

Sarah could detect the emotion beneath the cold front. She wanted to give him the opportunity, and the permission, to let it out.

"No, Jack. Things don't just happen. There's a reason. Everything happens for a reason."

He laughed.

"What?"

"That's a load of limp wristed hippy shit."

"What is?"

"My wife didn't die so that I could become a thief."

"I didn't mean it like that."

"Then what?"

She let him go and sat down. "Have you got a picture of her?"

Jack went over to the boxes. A moment and he opened one. He stood debating with himself whether or not to show Sarah his wedding album. He took the book out of its red velvet bag and looked at the golden lettering, remembering the day they had picked it out. He smiled at the stains from when Elisabeth had told him a joke and coffee flew out of his laughing mouth. He smiled at the memory of friends who had recommended cleaning fluids, and his and Elisabeth's refusal to have it cleaned. "Never," they had proclaimed. "This stain is a witness to joy!"

He looked at Sarah and saw his wife. He passed her the book.

"Thank you." Sarah opened the book and saw herself. The happy couple stood outside Tremont Street Church. They looked like they had just stepped off the set of Miami Vice. A shadow split the photograph in two, but it was Jack who stood in darkness, while Elisabeth shone, her face filled with love.

Until she saw the photograph, Sarah had hopes of something happening between herself and Jack, and although she knew she had awoken similar hopes in him, she also knew it would never work. She looked at Jack sitting on the couch opposite. His eyes narrowed and he withdrew into himself, studying her reactions, waiting for her response.

Sarah closed the book. "She's very beautiful."

"Yes." He reached over and took the album from Sarah. Jack had not looked at these photographs in God knows how many years. He opened the album and flipped through the pages, giving each image only a cursory glance. The last picture was of Jack and Elisabeth at their wedding reception, surrounded by the friends whom, in the months and years since her death, Jack had made a point of alienating. Now he relived the first dance to *Wind Beneath My Wings*, which they claimed to have picked because it was cheesy. Recalling the song now, Jack wanted to cry. He searched for some memory to cancel it out and found the maid of honor stepping up onto the stage.

She turned her back to the wedding guests and tossed her garter over her shoulder. The garter flew in a wide arc over upturned heads, outstretched arms, and hit Jack straight between the eyes. He dropped his drink and staggered backwards. The glass exploded on the floor. The guests turned away and turned again to look at the foaming beer. The maid of honor looked on, scarlet, while Elisabeth tended to Jack and a ring of stunned and curious people gathered around the garter. For a moment, it could have been an unexploded bomb.

Jack picked up the blue lace projectile and examined it. He found a penny twisted into the ribbon. Helen, the maid of honor, came sheepishly through the crowd.

"I'm sorry. I was aiming for Peter."

"It's OK." Jack laughed. "No harm done."

Helen turned, doe-eyed, to a middle-aged man who seemed to offer only hostility. Peter was actually in the grip of perpetual panic, but nobody ever realized this. He was one of Elisabeth's friends. Jack turned to Peter; he put up his hands and backed away, blowing a long comical "Noooo." Jack turned back to Helen and held out the garter.

"Promise me you'll never pitch for the Celtics."

"I promise." Helen's eyes were still fixed on Peter.

The memory served its purpose and Jack closed the album. He put it back into the bag and returned it to the box.

"So, what happens now?" he asked.

"Between us?" There was no need to say more. Both of them knew that nothing could happen while Jack was married to a dead woman.

Sarah picked up her jacket and put it on. "I have to go."

Jack gave her a smile filled with loss. He walked her to the door and opened it. They stood for a moment in the hallway.

"What are you going to do now?" he asked.

"I have something I need to take care of." There was something tragic about her as she turned and walked away. He watched until she turned the corner.

Jack closed the door and went back into the living room. Then he realized where Sarah was going.

19/Home Again

A flash of lightning split the sky and thunder rumbled in the clouds above the Whitely Museum. Jack Higgins, crouching just inside the perimeter wall of the Whitely Estate, wondered if the castle ever experienced any other kind of weather. He pushed the thought aside. Somewhere on the estate, he knew, Sarah was getting ready to face-off against the old man.

In the far distance, the lights of a truck turned in a wide arc and began the mile or so journey to the castle.

As he sat watching, Jack saw two men leave the castle and make their way to some old out buildings. Hugging the wall, Jack made his way along until he was directly opposite a vast metal barn. A dim light burned somewhere inside; he could make out the shapes of crates stacked to the ceiling. The frost in the air, the chill on his face, caused Jack's body to shake suddenly. He crouched down and covered his nose and mouth with a surgical mask to hide his breath. He had no plan, no idea of what he was going to do, he just had the sense that Sarah was in some kind of danger. Whether or not he could help her was another matter, but he was damned if he was going to sit back and do nothing. He had a vision of himself killing the bad guy and saving the damsel in distress. It was an image he found ludicrous, but he held onto it now like the adventure stories of his childhood, and the better world they promised.

The truck turned, and a faint light moved towards the

trees. Jack dropped to the ground as the full beams turned on him. Did the truck stop? There was a moment when he was certain it had, then the truck turned again and returned Jack to darkness. It came to a stop outside the barn. Two men climbed down from the cab and went around to the back. One of them knocked on the doors, bringing the echoing clang of an empty container to Jack's ears. The guard grabbed the handle, pulled on it and swung the door open. A burst of machine gun fire sent him scrambling for cover.

A terrified voice called from inside, "Throw your guns out where I can see them."

"Charlie, I'm gonna split your fuckin' head open when I get you."

"You were supposed to give me the code word."

At the side of the truck, the two guards looked at each other. This was the first either man had heard about a code word. As they argued, a voice called from behind, "Throw your guns out." They turned to see an old man crossing the yard. "Yes sir, Mr. Whitely." They threw their weapons out in view of the back of the truck.

"Charlie?" It was Whitely who spoke. "You recognize my voice?"

"Yes Sir."

"Good. I'm coming round so don't shoot me." With his hands in the air, Whitely walked around to the open door and reached up to Charlie.

"They were supposed to give me a code word Mr. Whitely."

"That's OK, Charlie. Help me up."

Charlie helped Whitely climb into the container, and then stood waiting for his reward. Whitely paused to catch his breath. He adjusted a signet ring on his right index finger, and then smashed his fist into Charlie's temple. There was a loud crack as pain and confusion registered on Charlie's face. He collapsed. Whitely picked up the gun and fired a single shot into Charlie's head, then called to the others,

"What are you waiting for?"

The two men came around and surveyed the scene.

"Help me down." When he was back on the ground, the old man issued his orders. "Get that inside and get rid of him."

"Yes Sir."

Whitely went back to the barn. The two guards retrieved their weapons and climbed up into the container. A minute later, they pushed a wooden crate to the edge and jumped down. With the crate slung between them, they followed their boss.

Jack edged his way towards the truck, staying hidden until the last possible moment, and then made a run for it. His first footfall on the gravel sounded loud enough to wake the city. There was nothing for it now but to keep going. He propelled himself up into the open mouth of the container and was confronted by Charlie's body. Half of his head was missing. Blood, bone and brain spread out in a pattern of gruesome beauty. The submachine gun lay in the middle of this. The barrel of the gun was crisp with burnt on blood. A mouthful of vomit landed on the corpse almost before Jack felt his stomach heave. He turned away and threw up again. He wiped his mouth and turned to the gun caked in blood. He was almost afraid to pick it up, but he needed a weapon.

Warm blood fell like syrup from the gun as Jack made his way to the barn. He stood at the door and peered in, searching for signs of life in the valley of crates. Harsh white light spilled from the centre and brought with it the sounds of celebration. Carefully picking his way, Jack followed the sound until he was almost upon them. Through a gap between two stacks of crates, he watched Whitely raise a glass in toast to someone out of sight.

"Be very careful moving that." Although he could not place it, Jack recognized the voice. He heard the sound of the guards at work and no prizes for guessing what they were carrying. Now Jack remembered the voice. It belonged to the old man who had called himself de Valfierno. Jack began to move towards the exit. He could hear the guards coming, and then stop. He waited, breathless in silence. After a moment, he heard their footsteps retreat. He began to move again. Sarah must be in the castle.

Jack turned a corner and almost slammed into the barrel of a gun. He shouted and jumped back, swinging the machinegun up, ready to fire. His face locked into Sarah's. She raised a finger to her lips and then pointed to the gun. Jack looked down and saw the trail of blood. Two months earlier, he would not have been that stupid. He bent down to place the gun on the floor.

"Don't move." Two guards were approaching, their guns trained on Jack. He started to turn the machine gun towards them. One of the guards fired, the bullet ricocheted off the floor by Jack's hand, sending a little cloud of concrete and dust up into his eyes. His hands flew up in surrender. He forced himself not to look towards where Sarah was moving out of sight. The guards came up to Jack, grabbed him roughly under his armpits and pulled him to his feet.

Whitely walked around the intruder, taking him in. Jack had expected to find madness in the old man's eyes. Instead, there was intelligence and a cool appraisal of what was before him.

Without taking his eyes off Jack; Whitely summoned de Valfierno. He came over; no longer blind, was anything true in this world? His eyes widened and his head turned to Whitely. Something between the two men gave Jack an idea. He called up all the contrition he could, and silently offered it to de Valfierno.

Whitely smiled, then turned away and began walking towards the exit. De Valfierno started to follow, but Whitely held up his hand. "You're going with them."

The guards led Jack and the old man back to the room.

One of the guards issued instructions to de Valfierno. He picked up a roll of duct tape and used it to secure Jack to a chair. The lead Guard then turned to de Valfierno. "Your turn."

"What?"

The old man's face tightened as it dawned on him what was going to happen. He looked hopelessly about. He tried to make a run for the exit, but he was too old. The sound of the gunshot bounced off the galvanized roof, and the metal containers, filling the room like an explosion. De Valfierno fell with a bullet in his back. One of the guards walked over and kicked him. "He's gone."

The guards picked up the Mona Lisa and started walking through the valley.

Whitely's study was filled with books he had never opened. The pristine spines of hefty volumes surrounded the desk built by a master craftsman and modeled on that of the American President. Behind the desk, a great stained-glass window depicted the death of Saint Sebastian. Whether Whitely saw himself as the saint or the arrows is open to debate. On the opposite wall, there was an empty space surrounded by trophies, skulls, daggers, snakeskin, a dried piranha, spears, and a jar of cloudy liquid, its contents long forgotten and unrecognizable after so many years.

Whitely came into the room and sat behind the desk. A computer screen in front of him flashed a message letting him know he had mail. He clicked the link. His face paled. He read of the war that had broken out in the small South American country where his primary business interests were held. Whitely Industries had just gone up in flames. The President had imposed Martial Law, and the army was marching on the barrios, killing anyone who refused to return to their homes. All of this had happened in that last half hour.

The President had come to power after his country's first

democratic elections. At that time, he was a young man studying economics in the United States. When they and Great Britain decided that an overwhelming majority of the young student's countrymen had elected the wrong man, the two countries agreed that, in the interest of freedom, he would have to be replaced. The order was drawn up and signed, and a team dispatched to dispatch the President. The young economics student found himself at the head of a very wealthy country, and promised new elections once things had settled down.

During his fifty years as interim head of the government, tens of thousands of people were disappeared. Some escaped; many more were killed trying to escape. For the past number of years, the government was financed, almost exclusively, by the National Endowment for Democracy, men like George Whitely and criminal accounts, like Jack's, made up the shortfall.

Some who survived the torture disappeared into the barrios, and it was one of these people, Jose Rodriguez, who was now trying to lead the country back to freedom.

On New Year's Day, The President will escape to a suburb of Washington, and spend the remainder of his life attending only the most fashionable receptions, and earning fifty thousand dollars a night as an after dinner speaker.

Whitely clicked to a news channel, President Bush was addressing the nation to condemn the uprising and declare Rodriguez a terrorist. Britain echoed America, and together they pledged to restore democracy to those *noble, freedom-loving people*.

Whitely switched the computer off; he slumped back in his chair, and his hands fell heavily into his lap. There was no need for stock checks, billions of dollars had just been wiped off the value of his company. As trading began around the world he would lose more money, and the banks, that had supported him for so long, making no attempt to collect on loans while the money was there, would now comb through his assets and find that even if they sold everything, Whitely would still owe them. He reached into one of the desk drawers. Suddenly his head turned in nervous confusion to the door. Was that a knock? It came again.

"Come." His voice was barely audible. The door opened, and the guards carried in the painting. They could feel death in the air, but they had no sympathy for the old man who now looked like one of his own relics. He swung a hand up to the empty space before him. Without a word, the guards hung the Mona Lisa in the waiting space. They stood back and turned to Whitely; he dismissed them with a wave of his hand.

She enthralled his eyes; he sat for a moment looking at her, then came round from behind his desk and stood before his latest acquisition. He reached to touch her flesh. He felt a sharp pain in his chest. He breathed deeply; his face relaxed and he was warmed by a sense of satisfaction. He went back behind the desk and sat down. He straightened his jacket and again reached for the drawer and again he was interrupted by a knock at the door. This time the interruption did not wait for an invitation. As the door began to open, Whitely was suddenly filled with rage. He flung open the drawer.

"You bought it?"

Whitely's head flew up to Sarah at the door. His eyes followed her's to the painting.

"Alice?"

Sarah quickened. "You know my name."

"Your name is what I tell you it is."

"Tell me about Peter Hopkins."

The name stopped Whitely. It unlocked something.

"Mom told me," Sarah said.

Whitely reached into the drawer; it was empty.

"I have it." Sarah held up the gun.

Whitely slumped down in his chair, "What do you

want?"

"I have something for you." She handed over a thick white envelope. Whitely looked at the handwritten address and wondered what it had to do with him. He looked at his daughter. She stood waiting. He opened the envelope and spilled its contents onto the desk. It was an old hardback book. He turned it over to look at the front. He opened the book and looked at the details. He smiled, and for the first time in her life, Sarah saw joy in his face. The book was from the first print run of *Frankenstein*. Whitely turned a page and was filled with horror: there, beneath the title, in red ballpoint pen:

Dear George,
I so hope you recognize the hand. I recall every instant of our acquaintance, every word, every look, every gesture you gave to me. Without you, my life would have been impossible.
The painting you are looking at is genuine. By now, you will know what has happened, and my dear, beloved daughter will finish the job. I just wanted you to know; I did it all for you.

All my heart's wishes I send to you now,
Peter Hopkins

The words worked their way through the old man's life and returned with the face of the boy. Whitely exploded, "Who the hell do you think you are?"

Sarah raised the gun. As she began to move round to Whitely, the old man started to move around to the front of the desk. They stopped, facing each other across the expanse of the room. Whitely raised his hand and began to reach inside his jacket. Sarah squeezed the trigger. The pain that tore into Whitely threw him back against his trophy cabinet, setting off a chain reaction that rattled his acquisitions, and ended with a loud smash as the specimen jar broke open at his feet. He looked at the thing that seemed to crawl from the mucous liquid, trying to identify it. He held up a hand in supplication. Again, Sarah squeezed the trigger and again Whitely was wracked by pain. Sarah squeezed the trigger a third time and behind her the great stained-glass window shattered, falling down like a veil as something large and white hit it. Instinctively Sarah turned away to protect herself. Whitely, in a final spasm of pain, fell to his knees, his face rose towards the figure given life by the storm; a monstrous apparition stepping through the broken night. A look of calm understanding came to the old man. He died.

Jack stood surveying the scene. Whitely lying dead and still reaching inside his jacket. Sarah with the gun at her side, staring astonished at the splinters of poplar centered on three bullet holes. She turned to Jack. There was blood trailing down the side of his face. He went over to Whitely's body to see what he was reaching for. He unbuttoned the jacket and let it fall open. Clutched in the dead hand was a check book.

"He always said money can get you anything," Sarah said.

Jack and Sarah looked at each other, not sure what to do next.

"Masterson wrote to me," Sarah said. She took a letter from her pocket and handed a few pages to Jack.

Peter Hopkins – VI

One night, when he was eighteen years of age, Peter Hopkins was on his way to meet Susan, his first real girlfriend.

They had met in the same bookstore where Peter first heard poetry. The night he met Susan, Peter was one of the readers, and afterwards, she had criticized the darkness of his work. Later, sprawled on his ratty sofa bed, they shared a joint, and she began quoting Sappho and Sylvia Plath. Suddenly she sat up, and Peter's jaw dropped at the magnificence of her breasts. He knew he was supposed to be above that sort of thing, but, *damn!* She raised her arms and waved them, letting the rhythm pour through her body. She closed her eyes and rolled her head, moaning. As suddenly as she had started, she stopped. She looked Peter in the eye and said, *'To live is to love is to give is to be free.'* The following morning he woke up with a poem in his head.

Believe we are born
To live simply and with love
In the world at hand.

Now, six months later, he was bringing her an advance copy of his first poetry collection: *Songs of the Pilgrim Soul.* The book was also the inaugural publication of a friend's small press.

Peter did not notice the car slow down. But after a few minutes he realized that it was keeping pace with him. He cast a sideways glance and saw one of the black windows roll down. A voice called from inside the car. "There's something I want you to see."

Peter recognized Whitely's voice. He got into the car, afraid that his scholarship was in danger of being whisked away.

"You write poetry. I saw something I thought you might enjoy." They drove in silence for a while. "How have you settled into college life? The Dean tells me you could become one of the star students."

"Yes, sir. Thank you. It's an excellent opportunity. I don't want to waste it."

They turned off the main road and up towards a cemetery. Once inside the gates Whitely turned off the engine. "Come on," he said and got out of the car. He led Peter a short distance away. "Here we are." He pointed to a grave. "I saw this and thought of you."

Peter read:

R I P

Philip Masterson
1885 - 1910

Here lies the body of Masterson, Phil,
Famed for the length and the breadth of his skill,
After he died,
We learned Phil had lied,
In his youth, he had broken his quill.

He laughed.

Whitely said, "My wife is pregnant."

Peter offered his congratulations. Inside he was both thrilled and terrified that the child was his.

"I thought you should know you did something useful with your life."

Peter slowly turned in dread, not at the words, but the tone. At that moment, Whitely pulled a knife and jammed the blade into the young man. As he fell, his sponsor explained, "Don't worry, I'm not going to kill you. You're on my team."

Whitely crouched down and dropped his knife. He took a pair of gloves and a plastic bag from his pocket. He put the gloves on, then picked up the knife and cut away the front of Peter's trousers, hacked away his sex organs and put them in the bag.

"I'm sorry to have to do this, but, I can't have children, so neither can you. You understand. I have an empire to consider. I have to be the father of that child."

Whitely stood up; he smiled sadly for what life had forced him to do, and then he walked back to the car, swinging his trophy in the plastic bag at his side.

The last thing Peter noticed before losing consciousness was the name: Masterson.

About the Author

Anthony Chapman was born in Ireland in 1969. Amongst other jobs, he has worked as a kitchen porter, a janitor, a tour guide, as a general labourer in construction, and as an actor. His only claim to fame is that he was a stand-in for Eric Idle on the movie *Ella Enchanted*

The *Heart & Mind* symbol is based on
a woodcarving I made in the late
1990's.

It's available on a t-shirt from
www.fergusanthony.com

Made in the USA
Charleston, SC
11 May 2015